Cam knew what he

He should say and send her off to be some to him. Delilah was young, alone and obviously in trouble, but she was a fighter. She needed a break, and for whatever reason, he wanted to give her one.

"I'll pay you in cash," he heard himself saying. She stared at him and he added softly, "Trust me."

"Why should I?" Her eyes narrowed. "Nobody gives something for nothing. If you think I'm gong to sleep with you just because you helped me, think again."

Cam laughed. "Listen, sugar, you may not be jailbait, but you're way too young for me. All I need is a waitress. Take the job or leave it."

Her chin rose and she put out her hand. "I'll take it. Thanks."

Dear Reader,

Several readers have asked me when the next BROTHERS KINCAID book was coming out. While this story isn't about one of the Kincaids, it is connected with the series, since the hero, Cameron Randolph, is a brother-in-law of the Kincaids.

You me him first in *Trouble in Texas* and again in *A Marriage Made in Texas*. Now, in *Somewhere in Texas*, Cameron Randolph's story unfolds.

Cam is the eldest of four. He's the one they all depend on, the one everyone turns to. The one with a soft spot for any stray that comes around. So even though he's a cynic where women are concerned, when a clearly desperate young woman breaks in to his place one rainy night, he knows he's going to help her.

The violence of the gulf storm that forced Delilah into hiding in Cam's back room is nothing compared to the danger from which she's fled. A secret she dare not reveal to Cam—a force that sent her life spiraling out of control… and may reach out to threaten the tough but tender man who offers her help, passion and maybe even love.

I love to hear from readers. Write me at P.O. Box 131704, Tyler, Texas 75713, egaddy@cox-internet.com, or visit my Web site at www.evegaddy.net.

Sincerely,

Eve Gaddy

Somewhere in Texas
Eve Gaddy

HARLEQUIN®

TORONTO • NEW YORK • LONDON
AMSTERDAM • PARIS • SYDNEY • HAMBURG
STOCKHOLM • ATHENS • TOKYO • MILAN • MADRID
PRAGUE • WARSAW • BUDAPEST • AUCKLAND

ISBN 0-373-71276-6

SOMEWHERE IN TEXAS

www.eHarlequin.com

Printed in U.S.A.

This book is for Katherine Garbera, who put up with me through all my tortured ramblings over the past two years, and who is probably at least as happy as I am that I'm writing again. Thanks for everything, Kathy.

A special thanks to Trana Mae Simmons and Rosalyn Alsobrook for helping me with so many research questions. And for being there for me.

As always, many thanks to my family for loving me, supporting me and putting up with me. I love you all.

Books by Eve Gaddy

HARLEQUIN SUPERROMANCE

Don't miss any of our special offers. Write to us at the following address for information on our newest releases.

Harlequin Reader Service
U.S.: 3010 Walden Ave., P.O. Box 1325, Buffalo, NY 14269
Canadian: P.O. Box 609, Fort Erie, Ont. L2A 5X3

CHAPTER ONE

THUNDER ROLLED, a deep, crashing bass. A jagged tear of lightning rent the sky and the wind shrieked an ear-splitting whistle. Cameron Randolph had seen and heard it all before. After living on the Texas coast all his life, a hurricane, or a storm close to it, was nothing new. Even so, he was glad to pull into his carport after the deluge started.

Cam's waterfront restaurant, the Scarlet Parrot Bar and Grill, was one of the most popular hangouts in Aransas City. Which, considering the town was the size of a flea bite, wasn't saying much. They closed at ten during the week, and on the weekends as well. Mondays he closed all day. Cam had discovered early on that even a single workaholic needed a day off every week, or he risked going crazy.

He came in through the carport entrance and up the back stairs, as he usually did. Instead of continuing up another flight of stairs to his apartment above the restaurant, he took a detour through the restaurant kitchen and on into the main dining room and bar area.

Crossing the wide planked floor to the hostess station, he grabbed a flashlight from beneath it in case the power went out. Which nine times out of ten during a bad storm, it did. He headed unerringly for the bar and switched on a light, but left most of the room in shadows. It seemed reasonable, since his mood was nearly as dark as the weather.

He made it a policy not to drink alone. As a bartender, he'd seen enough people ruin their lives with liquor to know he didn't want to go down that road. But tonight was no ordinary night.

Tonight was his fortieth birthday. And he felt as alone as a man could get.

It had been his choice. His sisters had given him a "surprise" party and invited plenty of unattached females. There had been several, he knew, who would have been happy to come home with him. But he couldn't crank up the interest. Not even in the redhead with the supermodel's body who'd flirted with him all night. So he'd come back home alone, to try to figure out when and why his life had become so damn boring—and what the hell he was going to do about it.

He picked up a shot glass and a bottle of Wild

Turkey Tennessee sipping whiskey and came around to the customer side of the bar, seating himself on a bar stool in the dim gloom thrown off by the single light left burning.

Cam poured out a shot and toasted the invisible bartender. "To women," he said, and laughed. A fact known to very few people, tonight was also the twelfth anniversary of the night he'd found his fiancée in bed with another man. A man he'd thought was a friend of his. He hadn't been tempted since. To marry, that is. Janine's infidelity hadn't turned him off women, but it had sure as hell persuaded him he didn't want to get married.

He didn't hate women. He had two sisters and a mother he thought were pretty terrific, even if their matchmaking did make him nuts at times. But he'd never yet met a woman he'd trust as he did his family. And if you couldn't trust a woman, you sure as hell better not marry her.

Deciding he was getting maudlin, he turned off the light, took his bottle and glass with him and headed to the back, through the restaurant kitchen to go upstairs to the small two-bedroom apartment where he lived.

The building had three separate sets of staircases. One around back, unconnected to the restaurant, ran from top to bottom. His visitors used that, and sometimes he did for those times he didn't want to go through the Scarlet Parrot to get to his apartment. Another came up from the storeroom and continued to the apartment. The third was in front and led directly to the restaurant.

The apartment suited him. It was small, but since he lived alone that didn't matter. And the commute to work couldn't be beat.

The noise from the storm faded, as it sometimes did in preparation for getting worse. During the lull he heard a sound, coming from downstairs, maybe from the storeroom off the carport. He knew he'd locked up, so it couldn't be the wind blowing open a door. Well, hell, he thought. Just what he didn't need on a night like this, a break-in.

He set the bottle and glass down and looked around the kitchen, wondering if he should pick up something for protection. He kept a baseball bat underneath the restaurant bar, but he'd never had to use it. Occasionally, someone got rowdy, but he generally just tossed them out and didn't bother with the bat. He was big enough to handle most men. And if he couldn't, help was usually available.

He didn't keep a gun. For one thing, Aransas City had almost no crime; for another, he didn't much care for guns. He'd had all he wanted of firearms during his brief stint in the military.

Besides, the most likely visitor this time of night was an animal looking for shelter from the storm. Probably that stray dog he'd been feeding lately. It was wild and scared and wouldn't come near him but he'd caught glimpses from time to time when he set out the food.

He went down the stairs and flipped the light switch in the storeroom, but the last crack of lightning must have done its usual number on the electricity. He aimed the flashlight around the sparsely furnished room. There wasn't much to see except the metal shelves holding some of his stores of liquor and beer. No sense furnishing something that flooded as often as not, which is why he left the first few shelves bare. Just as he was about to go outside to look around, he heard another sound.

He crossed to the outside door, found it had been forced open, and closed it. Turning back around, he played the flashlight around the room one more time. A glimpse of movement caught his eye and he could just make out a shape in the far corner beneath the window.

"Come on out. If you want to rob me you won't get much. I deposit the cash every night."

He waited, but the figure didn't move. "The cops will be here in five minutes so unless you'd like to take it up with them—"

The man rushed him, heading for the door. Cam grabbed him, dropping the flashlight as they wrestled. Whoever he was fought like a wildcat, scratching at his face, pounding on him with balled up fists, but the intruder was small and slight and didn't do much damage.

Cam finally managed to subdue him, wrapping his arms around him from behind, beneath what felt like… He ran his hand down the front of a soaking wet sweatshirt and found a very feminine chest beneath it. "What the hell?"

She didn't answer. Instead, she turned and kneed him viciously, where it hurt most, and before he could recover from that, she kicked his shin, hard. Cam had sisters who knew how to fight dirty and though it had been years he still knew the moves. He held on and shook her, saying through gritted teeth, "You're not getting out of here so don't piss me off any more than you already have."

"Take your hands off me, you pervert."

Her voice was husky, smooth and dark as the night.

"Like hell I will. You're the one who broke in and tried to rob me."

"I don't want your damn money. I only wanted some shelter—" She broke off as a deep hacking cough overcame her. "Let go of me!" she said when she could speak again. "I just want to leave."

"I don't think so." His hand brushed her forehead. She was burning up. What was she doing, sick and out on a night like this? Surely even a thief would have better timing.

"Come with me," he said, in a tone that brooked no argument, and dragged her toward the stairs. Thief or not, he wouldn't throw a sick woman out in this weather. At least, not until he found out exactly what she'd been up to.

She fought him, hissing, twisting and kicking. He had the devil of a time moving her, but his curiosity as well as his temper was roused. "Listen, honey, I've got you so you might as well relax."

She did more than that—she collapsed in his arms. At first he thought she was faking it but when he picked her up her head fell back and her body was limp, and to top it off, she shivered convulsively the whole time he carried her up the stairs. He kept right on going past the kitchen, up the second flight of stairs to his quarters.

With one hand, he opened the door and tried the light switch, hoping the power was back on, but nothing happened. He dropped the woman on the couch, grabbed a blanket and threw it over her before he lit the candles he kept around for emergencies.

It was pretty cold out, and she was soaked to the bone, but he didn't think that should have made her pass out. Obviously, she was sick, maybe had pneumonia. He thought seriously about calling EMT, but a quick check told him the phone was out and he didn't have a cell phone. That meant he couldn't call his brother-in-law either. Jay was a doctor and even if he couldn't see the woman, he could at least tell Cam whether he should get her to a hospital.

Cam put his fingers to her neck and felt for her pulse, relieved to find it was beating strongly. He considered stripping her and putting her in some dry clothes but he didn't want her to come to and freak out. Besides, she looked young and just the thought of taking her clothes off made him feel like a dirty old man.

Instead, he pulled off her backpack and dropped it by the couch, got some aspirin and water and tucked the blanket around her, hoping she'd wake up soon. If she didn't, he might have to drive her to the hospital in the teeth of the storm.

Her long, dark hair was plastered to her head. Her skin was clear and looked baby soft, though at the moment it was flushed with fever. She'd be pretty if she wasn't sick and wet as a drowned rat.

"Poor kid," he murmured as he towel-dried her hair. "I wonder what you're running from."

SHE CAME TO SLOWLY, unsure of her surroundings. She coughed, trying to figure out where she was.

Her head was fuzzy from congestion, and she felt light-headed, but that was lack of food, she was sure. Her body shivered underneath a blanket. Another nightmare?

Head swimming, she sat up in a rush. No, worse. Not a nightmare but reality. There was a man sitting beside her. A man she'd never seen before. Then she remembered. Breaking in, trying to get out of the storm. The blessed relief of getting out of the weather, her wrenched shoulder a small price to pay for warmth and cover. But before she could get used to it, the man came down the stairs and found her.

She pulled the blanket close and shrank back, battling her cough. "Don't touch me. I know karate." Like her mama always said, when all else fails, bluff.

He laughed. "Sweetheart, you could be a black belt and you'd still be too sick to take me on. Are you crazy, running around in a near hurricane as sick as a dog?"

The candles didn't give off a lot of light but enough to tell he was big, blond and drop-dead good-looking. Ten or fifteen years older than her, she'd guess. Not as old as—no, she wouldn't think of him. She was in a bad enough spot without that. "Let me go. I swear I wasn't trying to rob you."

"So you say." He frowned as another coughing fit

shook her. "It's suicide for you to go out in this weather. I'm not sure you don't need to be in the hospital."

"No hospital," she choked out. God no, she didn't want any records. He could find her that way. "It's only a cold. I'll be fine."

He didn't say anything but handed her a couple of pills and some water. "Take this. It's just aspirin," he said when she hesitated.

"How do I know that?"

He stared at her a minute, then swore and reached for a candle, holding it close to illuminate the medicine. She read the reassuring print on the pills.

"See, just like I told you. Aspirin." He set the candle on the coffee table and frowned at her. "Not very trusting, are you?"

"Why should I trust you?" But she took the pills and drank the water thirstily.

"Mostly because you don't have much choice." He got up and pulled her to her feet.

She staggered and his arm came around her, holding her firmly, but not too familiarly. Strangely, the contact didn't scare her. Which was a good thing because she was too exhausted to fight him.

"Take a shower," he said, guiding her to a small bathroom. "I'll get you some dry clothes and leave them outside the door. We can talk after that."

She didn't argue, but she did lock the door. Maybe it was stupid to trust him but she figured he could have done whatever he wanted to her when she was passed out before. And the thought of a warm shower and dry clothes was too tempting to turn down.

When she finally got out of the shower, she found the clothes and her backpack beside the door. The jeans and T-shirt fit, more or less, and she wondered if he was married and if they belonged to his wife. What would she say to his dragging in a perfectly strange woman he'd thought was robbing them? Or maybe he wasn't married and he had some other way in mind for her to repay him.

"You're just paranoid," she told herself, and went out to find her mysterious host.

He was in the kitchen, doing something at the stove. The lights were still out, but he'd brought candles into the room. Her first impression had been right. He was good-looking, disturbingly so. He glanced up when she entered and said, "Have a seat. Soup will be ready in a minute."

"Why is the stove working when nothing else is?" she asked suspiciously.

"Gas," he said, and put a bowl in front of her with a healthy helping of crackers. "Too many storms around here to depend on electricity."

Chicken noodle soup and it smelled like heaven.

Was this guy for real? Realizing she was famished, she dug in.

He took the seat across from her, waiting patiently while she ate. When she slowed down, he spoke. "How long's it been since you ate anything?"

She shrugged, trying not to stuff the food in too quickly. "I don't know. A couple of days maybe." Longer since she'd had an actual meal. Money had been tight and she'd been living off an occasional candy bar or fast food. Before that, she'd stopped eating when she realized her food had been drugged. She took another bite, found she couldn't eat any more and put her spoon down.

"Why are you being so nice to me? Last meal of the condemned?"

He laughed, showing beautiful white teeth. "Nothing so desperate. I haven't called the cops, if that's what you're worried about."

"Why not? You said you thought I was robbing you."

He took the almost empty bowl and set it in the sink. "I changed my mind." Leaning back against the counter, he crossed his arms over his chest. "So, what are you running away from, Anne?"

In the half shadows he looked large and menacing. She felt a tinge of fear but did her best to ignore it. "How did you know my name?"

He held up her wallet. "I checked your ID when you were passed out."

Anger flared. She got up to snatch it from him but a wave of coughing swept her and she had to sit down and wait for it to subside. "You had no right to go through my things." Everything she had, and it was pitifully little, was in that backpack.

He tossed it to her. "Sure I did. I found you breaking into my place, intent on robbery for all I knew. On top of that, you look like a kid. I don't harbor runaways."

"I'm not a kid. If you saw my ID you know I'm over twenty-one." She had a moment of panic before she remembered her license was still in her maiden name.

"So it says. I'm a bartender. I've seen my share of fake IDs."

"It's not fake." She closed her eyes in despair. If he called the cops, they would have to file a report. Something traceable, the last thing she needed. Hadn't enough things gone wrong? Why did she have to pick Dudley Do-Right's place to break into?

"I didn't say it was." He smiled when she stared at him. "You look younger, but—" He shrugged. "I believe you're twenty-five, Anne. And I'm also sure you're running away from something."

"Don't call me that." She never wanted to hear

the name Anne again. Anne had died that night in Houston. She wasn't that same woman, would never be again. "Call me Delilah." Her mother's nickname for her.

"All right. If you want my help, Delilah, you need to come clean."

Come clean? No way in hell. "What does your wife think about you dragging strangers into your home?"

He sat down, getting comfortable in the seat next to hers. "Nice try. I don't have a wife. Besides, we aren't talking about me. We're talking about you. Who are you running from, Delilah?"

She didn't answer.

He leaned forward, his gaze never leaving her face. "Husband? Boyfriend?"

No way would she answer that question. The longer she remained silent, the grimmer he looked.

"The law?"

"Not the law. I swear." She resisted the urge to cross her fingers. For all she knew, the Houston cops were looking for her right now. But she didn't think so, or she wouldn't have gotten this far. Besides, she refused to believe she'd killed Avery when she'd pushed him down the stairs. She gulped, remembering. He'd been so still. Awfully still. But no, he was too evil to die so easily.

Her host didn't speak, he only waited. She tried distraction again. "What's your name?"

"Cam. Cameron Randolph."

"Delilah St. John," she said, and offered a hand. Delilah, she thought, liking the sound of it. It felt comforting. She could almost hear her mother saying the name, her voice full of love.

He shook hands, holding on a little longer than necessary and staring at her intently. "People tell me their problems all the time. I'm a good listener. Is it so bad you can't talk about it?"

God, he sounded so sympathetic. But she'd fallen for that before and it had been a disaster. Still, there were nice people left in the world, even if she hadn't run across any lately.

But this man had taken her in, given her food and shelter. Even when he'd believed she was a thief, he hadn't called in the cops. She owed him some explanation, but the truth was out of the question.

"Yes," she whispered.

"Yes, it's that bad?"

Throat tight, she nodded, fearing his response. "Are you going to throw me out? Or call the cops?" She coughed again and damned her luck for getting sick right now.

He shook his head. "Nope. I'm going to give you

my spare bed and some cough medicine. We'll talk more in the morning, when you're feeling better."

Just like that? Who was this guy, besides too good to be true? "Why? I could be——anybody. I could be a con artist waiting to rob you blind."

"You could be, but I don't think you are." He got up and stood beside her. When he reached for her she flinched, unable to help the automatic response. His fingers touched her jaw. Then her neck, very gently sliding over the bruises. "Who hurt you, Delilah? Your husband?"

She shook her head, squeezing her eyes shut to block the memories, glad she'd taken off the rings the instant she left his house. "I'm not—married," she said hesitantly.

Was it a lie if she wished desperately that it were true? She'd have divorced Avery if it had been possible. But it was hard to divorce a man who kept you a prisoner. That didn't matter now, though. Not if he was dead. And if he was still alive…he'd be looking for her. Next time she might not get away.

Cam didn't press her. He showed her a small, cluttered room with a bed and a dresser, lit a candle for her, then left her. A few minutes later he came back with water, aspirin, cough syrup and a T-shirt for her to sleep in.

Clutching the soft shirt, she resisted the urge to

rub it against her face. "Cam? Why are you being so nice to me? You don't even know me."

He shrugged. "My good deed for the month. Don't worry about it. Get some sleep. And be sure to put out the candle before you do." He started to go, then turned to look at her. "Delilah? In case I'm wrong, there's no cash in the restaurant and I sleep *very* lightly." He left her before she could think of an answer.

She shut the door, feeling as if she were in a dream. She looked for a lock but didn't find one, and strangely enough, that didn't bother her. She should have been more wary of him. No one was this nice to a perfect stranger. But she didn't have the energy or will to fight anymore. Both had drained out of her during the last few weeks.

Being on the run from a killer could do that to a person.

CHAPTER TWO

THE STORM WORSENED overnight. A hurricane hovered out in the Gulf but by the next morning landfall was predicted in Louisiana, not Texas. Unless the hurricane changed course, they wouldn't have to board up and evacuate. Given the storm's severity, Cam didn't intend to open for lunch and possibly not for dinner either. Which gave him plenty of time to find out what was up with his houseguest.

She was in trouble, that he knew. What kind remained to be seen. Somehow, he didn't think she'd be trusting him with the truth anytime soon, but he had time. Just now he had nothing but time.

"Hi," she whispered, coming into the kitchen. She'd brushed her hair and it fell in thick, dark waves to her shoulders. Instead of his sister's clothes, she wore what she'd had on last night, muddy jeans and a navy sweatshirt. Even the shapeless sweatshirt couldn't quite disguise the tidy figure. Dressed up she'd be a knockout.

But right now she stood by the door looking young, scared and poised for flight. "Thanks—" she croaked, then cleared her throat and started again. "Thanks for the room and the clothes and everything. I can't repay you right now but I can send you some money as soon as I get on my feet."

On her feet? She looked as if a gentle wind would blow her over. Probably still hungry, too. "Sit down and eat something." He set a bowl, cereal and milk in front of her.

"Thanks, but I don't—"

"Sit down," he said in the tone he used on his nieces and nephews when he meant for them to mind.

Eyeing him with resentment, she sat, setting her backpack on the floor beside her. "I'm only doing this because I'm hungry, not because you ordered me to."

Amused, he smiled at her. "Glad we got that straight. So, have you looked at the weather? You planning on swimming your way out of here?"

Frowning, she glanced out the window at the rain that continued to pour down and beyond, to the white-capped ocean. "I didn't think you'd want me here any longer than necessary. I can't figure out why you took me in."

Neither could he, exactly. He put a cup of coffee in front of her and sat down with his own. "Curiosity. You still haven't told me who or what you're running from, Delilah."

Her eyes met his, bleak as a winter's day. "You're better off not knowing."

"That depends. If you're running from the law—"

"I'm not," she interrupted. "I told you that last night." She took a sip of coffee and closed her eyes. "Oh, that tastes so good."

The bruise on her jaw had faded more than the marks on her neck, but both were still visible in the light of morning. Some bastard had tried to choke her and though Cam knew police brutality existed, he didn't believe any cop had done that to her. But if she was running from an abusive boyfriend, why the hell didn't she just say so? Why lie about it, or avoid talking about it?

"Do you really know karate?"

She stopped shoveling in cereal for a moment to look at him. "Sort of."

Skeptical, he waited.

"Okay, I know some self-defense."

Not enough, apparently, to save her from being choked. "If I was convinced you're not in trouble with the law I might be able to help you out."

Starting on her second bowl of cereal, she looked up at him suspiciously. "How?"

Her eyes were blue. A deep, indigo blue a man

could drown in. *Get a grip,* he thought. She's just a kid. But her eyes weren't those of a kid.

"Can you wait tables? My newest girl just quit on me and waitresses are hard to come by around here."

"You're offering me a job?"

"Yeah. How about it?"

The smile transformed her face from pretty to sucker-punch gorgeous. *Don't even think it, bucko,* he told himself. *She's way too young for you.*

"I'm the best waitress you'll ever have." The smile faded. "But I can't take the job."

"Do you have any better prospects?"

She shook her head and got up to take her bowl to the sink. "I can't be on your payroll. And since you strike me as an honest guy who wouldn't want any trouble..." She shrugged. "But thanks for the offer. It's very nice of you."

He knew what he should do. He should say adios, give her some cash and send her off to be someone else's headache. But she got to him. She was young, alone, and obviously in trouble, but she was a fighter. She needed a break and for whatever reason, he wanted to give her one.

"I'll pay you in cash," he heard himself saying. She stared at him and he added softly, "Trust me."

"Why should I?" Her eyes narrowed, becoming

hard and mistrustful. "Nobody gives something for nothing. If you think I'm going to sleep with you just because you helped me, think again."

He laughed. "Listen, sugar, you may not be jailbait but you're way too young for me. All I need is a waitress. Take the job or leave it."

Her chin lifted and she put out her hand. "I'll take it. Thanks."

They shook hands. She had a firm, decisive grip, not a wimpy girl grip like a lot of women had. "You can stay in my spare bedroom. Unless you've got any better ideas." He knew she didn't.

She lifted a shoulder. "Not so far. I'll pay you rent," she said. "It won't be very long. Just until I can find a place of my own."

He didn't bother to tell her that wasn't going to happen in Aransas City, and for sure not on what he could pay her. She'd find out for herself soon enough. "It's a deal, then. I'll show you around later but I won't open until the storm lets up and we get some power. In the meantime, you should go back to bed. You still sound sick as hell."

"I'm fine, now that I'm out of the storm." There went that heartbreaker smile again.

Damn, he was too old to fall for a smile. Too old to fall for her, period. He shook himself mentally. It had been too long since he'd been with a woman. Way too long.

She paused at the door. "Thanks. No, I mean it," she said when he waved it away. "I really appreciate what you've done for me. You won't regret it."

Right. He was already cussing himself for being a fool. And not because he thought she was going to rob him. "What about your name?"

"My name?"

"Yeah, your name. Are you going to use the real one or a fake one?"

She blinked at him. "I hadn't thought of that."

"How long have you been on the run?"

She didn't answer for a moment, then shrugging, she gave in. "A little over a week." Her teeth worried her lip. "I guess I have to change it. Can you call me Delilah Roberts?"

"No problem." She was still frowning, lost in thought. "You're new to this, aren't you?"

"Lying? Yeah." She nodded jerkily. "I don't lie very well."

"No? Funny, most women I know are pros at it." He would have said all women, except his sisters didn't lie. They were a damn sight too truthful, if you asked him.

"That's sad."

Cam shrugged. "That's life." He watched her go

and muttered, "What the hell have I gotten myself into?" A particularly loud clap of thunder answered him.

Whatever she called herself, she was damn tempting. And Cam had never been very good at resisting temptation. *She's too young for you,* he told himself. Unfortunately, his libido didn't give a good damn about that. He had a feeling he'd be repeating those words a lot over the next few days.

WITH THE BRUNT OF THE STORM past and the power restored, the Scarlet Parrot opened at four that afternoon. Even though she must have still felt lousy, Delilah insisted on working. She'd taken some medicine, though, and at least her cough was better. Cam didn't argue too much, since the cook and Martha Rutherford, his full-time help, were the only employees who showed up. And as usual after a storm, business boomed. Cam wasn't sure what it was about storms but they seemed to bring all of Aransas City into his place in their wake.

His brother Gabe came in to sit at the bar and pass some time. Cameron slid his usual draft beer in front of him. "You haven't been around for a while. Have you been on a fishing trip?"

Gabe was a professional fishing-boat captain and spent a lot of time out on the ocean. He had the perpetual tan and near permanent bloodshot eyes that went with working on the water. Just now his eyes were even more bloodshot than usual, and he looked tired. But then, he often did.

Gabe nodded. "Just got back from Port Lavaca for a tournament."

"How'd it go?"

He frowned and rubbed a hand over his face. "Lousy. But I've got another trip planned later in the week. Hopefully it will be better."

"Good luck," Cam said, knowing the slow season was fast approaching.

"Thanks." Gabe glanced around. "What is it about bad weather that has the locals crawling out of the woodwork?"

"Beats me," Cam said, and grinned. "But I'm not complaining."

"Who's the new waitress?" He whistled long and low. "She sure is a looker."

Cam paused while polishing a glass and frowned at him. "Her name's Delilah Roberts."

Gabe raised his eyebrows. "Is she your new flavor of the week?"

"No." That was what Gabe called the women Cam dated, with some justification, he had to admit. Cam didn't tend to date anyone for more than a month or two. Better that way, since he didn't intend to get serious about them. They didn't seem to mind. None of them were the serious type either.

He set the glass down and picked up another. "Unlike you, I don't rob the cradle. She's a kid who's down on her luck. I'm just helping her out."

They both turned to look at her as she took some orders across the room. Gabe shook his head and smiled knowingly. "She may be down on her luck but she's no kid, bro."

Gabe was sure right about that. Twenty-five was no kid, even if she did look younger. Luckily someone called him away just then so he didn't have to listen to Gabe speculate.

A short time later, Martha put in an order and said, "I don't know where you found that girl, but you need to keep her. She's the best waitress we've had in here since I started working for you."

"Don't get your heart set on it. I doubt she'll stay long."

Better for him if she didn't, that was for sure.

"The good ones never do." She picked up the loaded tray and walked off.

Clearly, Delilah had been a waitress before. She was fast, efficient, and even more than that, she seemed to enjoy it. Cam had employed a number of people who weren't bad at the job but who wanted to find a different one as quickly as possible. But if she liked being a waitress, then why had she left her last job? And how had she ended up broke, homeless, and running from something? Or someone.

A voice broke through his reverie. "Hey, Cam, how about a refill?"

He drew a beer and set the frosty mug in front of his brother. "Enjoy it while it lasts. That's it for tonight." Gabe always stayed with him if he had too much to drink but Cam didn't need his brother sleeping on the couch when he already had one houseguest.

Gabe paused in mid-sip. "Why? You got a hot date set up for later?"

"Nope." And probably wouldn't have for the foreseeable future. "But you're still not bunking here."

Another customer called to Cam before Gabe could question him further. After that he was so busy with the bar he didn't talk to his brother again until closing. Gabe was still parked on the same stool and he looked like he didn't intend to go anywhere.

Martha and Delilah had finished clean-up and were stacking chairs on the tables across the room, so Cameron began wiping down the bar. "What are you still doing here?" he asked Gabe. "I'm not driving you home."

"Not a problem." Gabe held up his nearly empty mug. "I've been nursing this one for the last hour. So, if you don't have a date, what's up?"

"Nothing." He knew he'd have to tell Gabe sooner or later Delilah was staying with him, but he didn't want to just then. For one thing, he doubted Gabe would believe he wasn't sleeping with her and that his only interest in her was platonic. *Platonic, my ass.* If she'd been a little older, if she weren't working for him...

But she wasn't older and she was his employee, so he might as well put that idea out of his mind.

"We're done, Cam," Martha said, coming over to the bar. "I'll make the deposit for you if you want."

"Thanks, I'll have it ready in a minute." He went to the register and started totaling the cash. Tomorrow he'd run the checks and credit-card receipts, but he liked to get most of the cash into the bank at night. The Scarlet Parrot had never been robbed but Cam didn't believe in tempting fate.

"Hello, handsome," Martha said to Gabe, who was one of her favorites. "I haven't had a chance to talk to you tonight. You found yourself a lady friend yet?"

Gabe grinned and winked at her. "Waiting for you, darlin'. When are you going to dump that husband of yours and run off with me?"

Martha laughed, like she did every time they went through the routine. Cam always wondered why neither of them got sick of it, but they didn't.

She called out to Delilah, who was sweeping the floor. "Come meet the boss's brother, Delilah." She elbowed Gabe in the ribs. "Pretty, isn't she?" she said in a stage whisper.

Delilah glanced at them but continued to work, coughing a little as she did so. "Let me finish sweeping."

"Cam can do that. It would be good for him to get some exercise."

"I don't mind." She continued sweeping for a few moments, then came to the bar.

Martha introduced the two. Cam had to go to his office to get the bank bag and deposit slip. When he came back to the bar, he didn't need a crystal ball to know Gabe had hit on Delilah and she had blown him off. It was clear as a bell from the strained atmosphere and the dirty look Delilah shot Cam when she saw him. Being a woman, she naturally blamed him for something he had no control over.

No surprise there. Gabe liked young, pretty women as much as the next guy. Even in jeans and a T-shirt, Delilah was something to look at. No, what surprised him was the irritation he felt for his brother and the strong urge he had to protect Delilah. Yeah, right. Protect her from Gabe so he could have her himself?

"Crash and burn, did you?" he asked Gabe.

"That is one unfriendly chick," Gabe said, watching her wash dishes at the sink in the bar. "I swear all I did was ask her how she liked it here and offer to take her fishing on her day off."

"You don't need to hit on every new employee I have." Which was a little unfair because Gabe didn't, usually.

"I didn't hit on her. I asked her if she wanted to go fishing. It's not a big deal." He tilted his head, considering Delilah. "Maybe she's gay."

Cam laughed. "Because she shot you down? I don't think so, Gabe."

Delilah walked over to him, holding a pitcher. "Where do you keep this?"

"Above the bar, but let me get it. You won't be able to reach it." One problem with his setup, it wasn't made for short people. He took the pitcher from her and hung it up.

"So, Delilah, where are you from?" Gabe asked.

"Around," she said shortly.

"Yeah, but where?"

She gave him a dirty look but she answered. "A little town north of here. You've probably never heard of it."

She didn't add anything. Most people would have dropped it when it became clear she didn't want to talk, but not Gabe.

"Hey, I know a lot of towns in Texas. Especially on the coast. Which one is it?"

"It's not on the coast." Delilah shot Cam an irritated glance, then shrugged. "Alice," she said, naming a small town to the west of them. "Do you know it?"

Cam winced. He and Gabe had driven through there not a month ago.

"Never heard of it," Gabe said, but he looked at Cam and raised his eyebrows.

Ignoring him, Cam handed Martha the money bag. She put her jacket on and turned to Delilah. "Need a ride, hon?"

"No, thanks, Martha."

Like Gabe, Martha never let anything go. "I know you don't have a car and we don't have any buses in this burg. It's no bother, let me give you a ride."

Delilah didn't answer. Her eyes met Cam's and he swore silently. "Delilah doesn't need a ride. She's staying here for now, Martha."

Gabe looked from one to the other. "Uh-huh. Now I get it. Why didn't you just tell me?" he asked Cam.

Martha looked surprised. "She's staying with you? Upstairs?"

"That's right."

"But you don't take boarders. At least, you never have before."

Gabe choked on a laugh. "None of them looked like Delilah, either."

"Shut up, Gabe." He glanced at Delilah and wasn't surprised to see her frowning. At the moment he'd gladly have fired Martha if it would have gotten her to shut up. But nothing ever shut Martha's mouth once she started. "Let it go, Martha."

"Well, okay. You don't have to tell me to mind my own business. I'm not one for gossip," she added in an injured tone. Her statement should have amused him, since Martha was undoubtedly one of the town's prime gossips, but somehow it didn't.

Gabe sent him a knowing smile that made Cam want to punch him. "Don't start, Gabe. It's not like that."

He spread his hands innocently. "Did I say anything?"

"You were about to."

Gabe stood. "Hey, it's none of my business."

"Yeah, you got that right." But that wouldn't stop Gabe from ragging on him.

"Come on, Martha," he said, taking her arm. "I'll walk you out. I think they want to be alone."

Martha shot them a speculative glance, but she let Gabe lead her away.

At the door he paused. "Come to think of it, Delilah, I have heard of that town." He scratched his head, looking puzzled. "But I thought Alice was about forty miles west of here. Not north. But hey, what do I know?" He waved and they went out.

Delilah stared at the closed door, then looked at Cam. "Shit. I told you I was a bad liar."

CHAPTER THREE

THERE WAS SILENCE for a long moment after Gabe and Martha left.

"Couldn't you think of a town that really *was* north of here?" Cam asked her.

Delilah propped her hands on her hips and glared at him. "Obviously not, or I would have said it. I wasn't expecting the third degree."

He snorted in disgust. "Or here's a shocker. You might have tried the truth. Houston's a big place, what would it have hurt?"

The truth? How could she tell the truth when it might land her in jail? Or worse, get her killed. "Where I come from is none of your brother's business."

"True." He locked the front door to the restaurant and turned out the lights. "But it is my business."

"You know I'm from Houston. You saw my ID."

"Yeah, but that's all you've told me. And you didn't tell me that. If I hadn't found your wallet I wouldn't know squat about you." He didn't say anything else, but walked into the kitchen, leaving her to follow.

She hated it, but he was absolutely right. Cameron Randolph had given her food, shelter, and even more importantly, a job. And she had repaid his kindness by lying. Not willingly, but she'd lied nonetheless. For a notoriously bad liar, she'd told a ton of them today. She wondered if it would get any easier, the more lies she told.

By the time she went upstairs, he'd gone into his bedroom and shut the door. Debating, she waited outside his door, then decided she couldn't leave things like they were. If nothing else, she needed to know if he was going to kick her out. As she raised her hand to knock, the door opened.

He stood in the doorway wearing jeans and nothing else. Though she told herself it was a mistake, her eyes were drawn to the broad expanse of his chest. Damn, he looked good. Shocked, she felt a tug of attraction.

Forget that, she told herself. Her instincts about men were obviously screwed up.

Cameron didn't look very happy to see her. He leaned a shoulder against the door jamb and frowned at her. "What do you want, Delilah?"

"I know you're mad at me and I can't blame you.

But I have a reason for—for not talking about my past." Fear. That was a very good reason.

"Lying isn't usually a good idea, no matter what your reasons are. Lies come back to bite you in the butt if you're not careful."

"I know." She bit her lip, wishing she could talk to him, but she couldn't risk it. "I'm sorry, I still can't talk about it."

"Because of this?" He laid his fingers gently on her neck, over the bruises that had finally begun to fade. "You're afraid of whoever did this to you."

This time she didn't flinch. His fingers were warm, his touch soothing. They stood close together, so close she could have laid her head on his chest. And she had a brief, insane urge to do it. She could smell him, a clean, masculine smell mixed with a hint of spicy aftershave. She could feel the heat from his body and the awareness simmering between them.

Their gazes locked and she almost leaned forward. What the hell was she doing? She drew back and his hand fell away, breaking the contact. "That's part of it."

Thank God, he looked irritated again. She could handle irritated. She couldn't handle sincere and kind and…oh, hell, sexy.

"Part of it, but not the whole story. You're not going to tell me the whole story, are you?"

She shook her head and braced herself, waiting for him to tell her to get out.

For a long moment, he simply looked at her, his gaze inscrutable. "Get some sleep," he said. "Sundays can be brutal." He shut the door in her face.

"Thanks," she told the closed door. At least he hadn't put her out on the street.

For the first time in over a week, no nightmare woke her in the middle of the night. A certain blond and very hot bartender figured prominently in her dreams, but she wouldn't complain. Anything was better than waking in a cold sweat, terrified for her life.

As CAM HAD PREDICTED, the lunch rush kept them busy. Delilah kept her ears open and her mouth shut and learned a lot about her boss and a number of other people she hadn't yet met. Apparently the Scarlet Parrot was one of the small town's hot spots.

Martha wasn't Cam's only employee who liked to talk. During the afternoon lull, Rachel, another waitress who came in part-time, gave her an earful of gossip as well.

Rachel, a frizzy-haired blonde, was nineteen and wore an eyebrow ring, a belly-button ring, and more rings on her fingers than Delilah had ever seen. At the moment, she was whining about the lack of single men in Aransas City.

"So I go to school in Corpus Christi and date like, the guys from around there but they all think Aransas City is like the Twilight Zone." She smacked her gum and picked up the dirty dishes from one of the tables as Delilah bused the one next to it. "Which it is. And the only available guys in town are geeks."

Delilah made a sympathetic noise and wondered if she'd ever been that young. If so, she couldn't remember it. Her mother had died when she was sixteen and she'd been on her own ever since.

"You think he's a geek?" Delilah asked, motioning at Cam. "He's single, isn't he?"

"Cam? Oh, I think he's a total hottie, but I meant guys my age. Besides, Cam dates really gorgeous women. You know the type, with boobs out to here," she said, waving her hands in front of her small chest. "I couldn't compete if I wanted to."

She cast a calculating look at Delilah. "You sure could, though. You'd have to do something about your clothes. They're pretty boring."

Delilah laughed. "Thanks, but I'll pass."

"Cam doesn't hit on his employees, anyway. Martha says it's a rule of his." She shrugged. "Which is kinda nice." She looked a little doubtful about that.

"I'll keep that in mind," Delilah said.

"Cam's got a brother," Rachel said, brightening.

"A younger brother. He's hot, too, but way different from Cam. He's a fishing-boat captain."

"Gabe? I met him last night." Gabe Randolph didn't much like her. Not that she blamed him. She hadn't been very tactful when she'd turned him down. And of course, the fact that she'd lied about where she was from and he knew it didn't help much either.

Rachel stopped working to look at her. "You didn't like Gabe? He's always been really nice to me."

"Other way around. He doesn't seem to have much use for me."

Which became abundantly clear just a little while later. Gabe came in and took a seat at the bar, in what was apparently his usual place. Delilah avoided him as long as she could but eventually had to pick up a tray at the bar where he was talking to Cameron. They were talking so intently neither of them noticed her.

"I just think you should be more careful about who you hire," Gabe said.

"Who I hire is none of your business," Cam replied. "Delilah isn't a problem."

"She's a liar, Cam. Do you even know where she's really from? Because it sure as hell isn't Alice." Cam didn't answer and Gabe continued. "Do you know

anything about her? Does she even have any references?"

"Since when are you so concerned with references? I've known you to take on deckhands with no
kind of history other than them swearing they don't
do drugs."

"At least I have a feel for if they're honest. She's
not, that's pretty damn clear."

Cam looked up and met her eyes. "You need to
give it a rest, Gabe."

Gabe turned around and looked at her. He wasn't
embarrassed to be caught talking about her. If anything, his gaze was even more unfriendly. He turned
back to his brother. "You're asking for trouble,
Cam."

Delilah didn't wait to hear any more.

Late that afternoon, Delilah was behind the bar
helping Cam stock up for the night. Cam had gone
downstairs to bring up another case of beer when a
woman came in carrying an infant seat. She walked
directly to the bar and set the seat on the floor, reach-
ing down to unbuckle the straps and pull a baby out
of it.

"You must be the new waitress," she said, holding the fair-haired child in the crook of her arm. She
held out her other hand. "Gail Kincaid. I'm one of
Cam's sisters. This is my son, Jason," she added,

smiling fondly as the baby kicked his legs and waved chubby arms.

"Hi, I'm Delilah," she said and shook hands. "Cam should be back in a minute. Can I get you a menu?"

"No, thanks. I'm waiting for my husband to meet me for an early dinner."

Delilah left her. A few minutes later, after Cam came back, she heard the baby crying. She watched him take the child from his mother and put him up on his shoulder, saying something that had Gail laughing. In no time at all the baby quit crying and started chortling.

Cam plainly liked children and was good with them. From what Martha and Rachel had said, he was close to his family. She gathered that all of his siblings dropped by his place often. He was a good boss, too. Every single one of his employees she'd talked to thought he was great.

So why wasn't this piece of masculine perfection married? And why in the world was she so curious about him? After all, it was none of her business. She wouldn't be around long enough to find the answers, either.

CAM HANDED HIS NEPHEW back to his sister. "That kid has some set of pipes. But then, all your kids are loud," he said, remembering Gail's daughters at the same age. "And speaking of all your kids, how are the little darlings and why haven't they been in?"

"Mel and Roxy are great. They're with Barry this weekend," she said, referring to her ex-husband. "And they were in last week."

He put a glass of iced tea in front of her. "Talk to Gabe this morning?"

She tried to look innocent, without success. "Just for a minute. Why do you ask?"

"Because," he said as he leaned forward and flicked her cheek, "I know Gabe and I know you. Besides, Gabe's already been in and couldn't find anything out, so he's bound to try to see if you can do any better. Am I right?"

"All right, I admit it. He wanted me to come pump your new waitress for information."

"Naturally, you went along with him."

"No, but he did make me curious about your new help. I didn't think you'd mind if I came in to meet her for myself." She glanced across the room at Delilah, then back to Cam. "Gabe says she's living with you. A little younger than most of your women, isn't she?"

He gritted his teeth, thinking of ways to get even with his brother. Who the hell did he think Cam was, James Bond? "Delilah is not one of my women. I let her stay in the spare bedroom. She's in a jam and has no place to go."

"If you say so." Gail looked at Delilah again. "She's very pretty. Are you sure you aren't interested in her?"

"Sure as hell's hot and a Popsicle's cold," he assured her. *Liar, liar.* He hadn't slept well the night before. Instead, he'd lain awake thinking of her. And after he finally did manage to sleep, he'd woken up this morning hard as a rock.

She was pretty. No, she was beautiful, but he'd had his share of beautiful women. What was it about Delilah that got to him? Because she was in trouble?

Jay came in and, seeing them, walked over to the bar. "Hey, Cam." He kissed Gail and took his son from her. "I'm in desperate need of the shrimp plate," he told Cam as he sat beside Gail and settled the baby in his arm.

"You're always in desperate need of the shrimp plate." He glanced at Gail. "Which I can't order for you because Gail here is too busy yammering at me. Can't you keep your wife under control?"

Jay gave a bark of laughter. "No. One thing I've learned is never to get in the way of Gail and her family."

"Men should stick together," Cam said.

"Sorry. She's a lot prettier than you are. Besides,

I sleep with her." He leaned over and kissed her smugly smiling mouth.

"How old is Delilah?" Gail asked. "Last question, I swear," she said when he frowned at her.

Not if he knew his sister. "Twenty-five."

She looked at her husband and smiled. "Jay's younger than me and we get along fine. You know, Cam, it wouldn't be a crime if you *were* interested."

"I'm not," he said, and tried to mean it.

IT WAS CLOSING TIME before Delilah had a chance to talk to Martha again. "Do you know of any apartments for rent?" Delilah asked her. "Or even a room would do. It just needs to be cheap."

Martha laughed. "Oh, honey, there are slim pickings in this town. The only apartment complex near Aransas City is full up and overpriced to boot. You best stay here and be glad you've got a place to park yourself."

As soon as everyone left, Delilah rounded on Cameron. "Why didn't you tell me there wasn't any place to rent here? I told you I was going to look for another place and you didn't say a word."

He glanced at her, then went back to totaling receipts. "What difference does it make? Don't forget, I looked in your wallet. You can't afford another place anyway. I told you, you can stay here."

*I'll take care of you. You won't ever have to worry
again.* The words haunted her. What if she'd never
gone out with Avery? Never listened to his smooth
lies? Fallen for those practiced moves? For damn
sure she wouldn't be in the fix she was in now.

"That's it. I'm out of here." She ripped off her
apron and threw it at Cam. "Keep my pay. It should
cover the room and board for the last two nights."

He stared at her and frowned. "Don't be stupid,
Delilah. It's eleven o'clock on a rainy Sunday night
and you've got twenty bucks and no place to stay.
Except right here."

*No place to go. No one who cares. You're alone…
alone…I'm all you have…All you'll ever have…
You're mine…You can't survive without me…You'll
never leave me.*

Sweat popped out on her forehead. Her stomach
roiled, her throat closed up. Dizziness hit her like a
sledgehammer. The words jumbled and a roaring
sounded in her ears.

The next thing she knew, Cam had pushed her
into a chair and shoved her head down between her
knees. Dimly, she heard him curse and leave her.
Seconds later, he came back with a paper bag.
Gratefully, she snatched it from him and breathed
into it, head still between her knees.

Slowly, she gained control and the dizziness left.

She knew she was overreacting. Big time. But she couldn't help it. Cam's words had triggered her worst fears. Nightmare visions that were all the more horrifying because they were real, not imagined.

Cam had crouched down beside the chair and was studying her, his expression troubled. "Better?"

She sat up straighter and nodded shakily. "Yeah. Sorry I flipped out."

"You want to tell me why you freaked?"

"I can't." She wanted to, but she was afraid. Afraid he wasn't as good as he seemed. Afraid her story would sound crazy. No one would believe a well-respected attorney was the cruel monster she knew him to be.

Cam stood, pulled up a chair to sit in front of her. "Look, Delilah, it's obvious you're scared to death about something. You don't believe you can tell me. You don't know me and have no reason to trust me. But you need to tell someone, and I think it should be the cops."

She gave a slightly hysterical laugh. "I can't go to the cops." Why bother? It would be pointless, given Avery's connections.

"Then try me."

His eyes were unusual, a clear, dark gray fringed with black lashes. Beautiful eyes, which she sus-

pected he knew. According to everything she'd
heard, Cameron Randolph liked women, and they
liked him right back. She could see why. He was
very appealing. She found herself falling into the
sincerity of those eyes.

She pulled herself up in a hurry. What was she
thinking? She couldn't trust anyone, couldn't depend on anyone other than herself.

He put his hand over hers and squeezed it gently. "Were you raped? Is that what you're afraid to
tell anyone?"

Her eyes teared up as she shook her head. "It's
not that simple." She could hear Avery, telling her
she owed him her obedience. Obedience, for God's
sake, as if she were a dog and he her master. She remembered his smile and his promise to teach her respect, as he had his first wife.

His first wife. Oh, God, don't think about that.
She would lose it if she thought about what he'd
done to that poor woman. What she *suspected* he'd
done, she reminded herself. She had no proof, just
a journal from a dead woman and a gut feeling she
had to get out as soon as possible.

"Did he try, and you stopped him?"

"I can't talk about it. I ran away, all right? I got
out."

"I can't help you if you won't talk to me."

"He didn't rape me," she said flatly.

He looked doubtful. "He hurt you. Don't forget, I saw the bruises. You can still press charges."

No she couldn't. The Houston cops wouldn't believe her. Avery would see to that. And even if she tried, and went to them… No, it was too risky. "No."

"Damn it, Delilah, you can't let the scum get away with this. I'll take you to the police station myself."

"No!" She grabbed his arm, her fingers tightening on it. "I can't go to the police."

"Why not?"

"Because when I ran away—" It was crazy to trust him, insane to let this man she barely knew in on her secret. But she couldn't run anymore. And she had to trust someone.

"Just tell me. It can't be that bad."

"Yes, it can." She raised her eyes to his and blurted it out. "I think I killed him."

CHAPTER FOUR

FOR A LONG MOMENT, Cameron simply stared at her. "You killed him?" Of any number of things he'd expected to hear, that wasn't one of them.

"Yes. No. Oh, I don't know!" She sprang out of her chair and started pacing. "I shouldn't have told you. I can't believe I did. I've got to get out of here." She dashed out of the room.

He followed her up to the apartment. By the time he got there, she'd grabbed her backpack and was halfway to the door. He crossed his arms and stood in the doorway, blocking her way. No way would he let her leave now. There had to be more to the story than this bald admission of murder.

"Don't even think about leaving. You're not going anywhere until you tell me what happened."

She walked to the door, looking as if she wanted to shove him aside. "Get out of the way." He didn't move, or speak. "I told you, I might have killed a man. You could be harboring a murderer. Doesn't that bother you?"

She looked so young, and so desperately earnest. Whatever had happened, he'd bet his restaurant she was no cold-blooded murderer. He took her arm and pulled her back into the room. "Sit down. I'm going to get you a drink and then you can tell me what happened. *Exactly* what happened."

The fight drained out of her. "You're crazy," she said, but she sat on the couch.

He got out a couple of glasses, figuring he needed fortification, too. "Bourbon okay?"

"I don't care."

He brought the glasses and the bottle and set them on the coffee table, taking a seat beside her. She took her drink and knocked back the liquor with a quick twist of her wrist. He raised his eyebrows, then followed suit. He reached for the bottle and poured some more into her glass.

She picked it up but paused before she drank. "I'm not a lush," she said.

He didn't speak, just waited for her to begin.

Cupping the glass, she sat staring at it as she spoke. "The man I was…involved with wasn't the person I thought he was. I stayed with him, tried to make it work, but he just kept getting more possessive and controlling. Finally, after—" She looked at him, then shook her head. "It doesn't matter. I knew I had to leave him." She took another sip of bourbon, her fingers tightening on the clear glass.

She spoke slowly, with obvious effort. "He was angry. Furious. I'd never seen him like that. He started hitting me." She closed her eyes for a moment, as if gathering strength to finish the story. "He clocked me. Slugged me right on the jaw and I went out like a light. When I woke up he had locked me in a bedroom on the second floor."

"Son of a bitch! He locked you in?"

She nodded. "He had an alarm system on the window, so I couldn't have left that way without him knowing. He said he wouldn't let me out until I could 'be reasonable.'" She looked at Cam with no expression. "That's what he said. Be reasonable. I was supposed to be reasonable about him beating the hell out of me."

Cam wished he had just a moment alone with the bastard. He'd show him what it felt like to be beaten. But he didn't say anything, just waited for Delilah to continue.

"He kept me there for several days." Shuddering, she took a sip, then started again. "He brought me food, but after I passed out a couple of times I realized it was drugged. So I stopped eating. There was a bathroom attached to the bedroom, so I was able to have water."

Cam swore. "Then what happened?"

"He was careless, since he thought I was out of it. So when I saw my chance, I tried to get away. We fought again and I made it to the stairs but he caught up with me. He choked me. He said he should kill me for what I'd done. I kneed him and he dropped his hands for a minute and I—I pushed him down the stairs."

"Are you sure he's dead?"

Her eyes widened. "It was the back staircase. Steep and narrow. I thought he was dead. He was so still."

"But you didn't check."

"No, I grabbed my backpack and ran like hell. If he wasn't dead I didn't want to hang around to find out."

Okay, something concrete they could focus on. He set his glass down. "There's no sense blaming yourself for something that might never have happened. The first thing you need to do is find out if he's still alive."

"How am I supposed to do that?"

"Call him. That's the easiest way."

"No." She shook her head decisively. "If he's alive he could trace the call. I don't want him to have any way of finding me."

"You really think he's having the incoming calls traced? That seems kind of excessive."

She laughed humorlessly. "Yeah, well, he's an excessive kind of guy. I wouldn't put anything past him. You don't know him. You don't know what he's capable of."

Obviously, she wouldn't budge on this one, no matter what he thought about it. "Okay, no phone calls. We can go to the Internet. Check the papers and the obituaries. The restaurant's closed tomorrow and I've got some things to do, but we should have plenty of time to check it out." She didn't speak and he added, "If you want me to help, you'll have to tell me the guy's name."

"I don't want to involve you any more than I already have. It's not fair to you." She set her glass down, then stood to pace the room, rubbing her hands up and down her arms.

Somehow, he didn't think that was her main reason for refusing. "This guy really did a number on you. I can see why you wouldn't trust men easily. But you trusted me enough to tell me you might have killed him, don't you think you can trust me with his name?"

She shot him a worried glance. "There's more to the story than I've told you."

"Yeah, I already figured that out." They were

both silent while he watched her pace. "So, Delilah, are you going to trust me or not?"

She stopped pacing and looked at him. "What happens if I don't?"

He shrugged. "Then I can't help you."

"You won't—kick me out?"

"No. Why would I? It's your business, even if I think you're making things harder than they have to be, it's still your decision." As for harboring a murderer, she might have killed him accidentally but Cam didn't believe for a moment she'd murdered the scum.

She looked stunned, prompting him to ask, "You haven't had many breaks lately, have you?"

She laughed. "Not good ones, anyway." Her eyes met his and she smiled. "Until I broke into your place."

Oh, man, he was getting in deep when a simple smile zapped him. Maybe he just missed looking out for his sisters. Since they'd gotten married, they didn't need him to worry about them anymore. And Delilah clearly needed someone to look out for her. Except he didn't think about her like a sister. No way, no how.

She took a deep breath. "I can't tell you his name. I'm sorry, but I can't."

He was conscious of a pang of disappointment

that she wouldn't trust him. But she didn't know him, after all. He might not like it, but he could understand it.

She was watching him with an anxious look on her face. "Okay, if you won't, you won't. Sit down, Delilah. You look like you're about to keel over."

"Sorry. That liquor hit me harder than I'd thought it would." She sat and put her head in her hands. "I don't feel so good."

He wanted to touch her, to comfort her, which surprised him. He hadn't felt that way about a woman in a long time. But his protective feelings didn't worry him. They were as natural to him as breathing. No, the other things he was thinking about were what worried him. He was entirely too aware of her as a woman, rather than a kid who needed a break.

But she wasn't a kid, and that was the problem. "You need to eat. I'll make you a sandwich."

A short while later he came back with a peanut-butter-and-jelly sandwich and a glass of milk. She laughed when he set it in front of her. "Milk?"

"Drink it, it's good for you. You sure as hell don't need any more booze."

"You're right about that."

He said no more as she ate, thinking about what he could do about her problem.

"That hit the spot. Thanks," she said and got up to take the dishes to the kitchen.

He followed her. "You could check it out yourself on the Internet. I can let you use the computer. But why don't you wait until morning? You're wiped out."

She stared at him a long moment. "You're too good to be true."

He smiled. "It's not a big deal, Delilah. I wish you'd trust me, but if you can't..." He shrugged. "Anyway, one more night won't make any difference. You're still sick. Get some rest."

She looked exhausted, but he wasn't surprised when she stayed where she was.

"All right," she said reluctantly. She still didn't leave. "What if he's dead? What do I do then?"

He was afraid if he answered, she might bolt. But he wouldn't lie to her. "Then you go to the police."

Her shoulders slumped. "I was afraid you'd say that. You realize they'll toss me in jail and throw away the key. They'll charge me with murder."

"No, they won't." He didn't like her expression. Despair didn't sit easily on her. He crossed the room to her and took hold of her arms, but gently. "Delilah, if he's dead, then it was an accident. And you did it in self-defense."

She looked into his eyes, her own dark blue,

troubled, and deep as the ocean. "You believe me, but what if the police don't?"

"He beat you. He choked you. He kept you a prisoner, for God's sake. Why wouldn't they believe it when you've got the bruises to prove it? Besides, you'll hire a lawyer if you need to." He dropped his hands and started to turn away.

"Public defender. No money, remember? And I don't know about you, but I've heard horror stories about overworked public defenders."

"You're dreaming up worst-case scenarios about something that might not even be an issue. Try not to worry." Which was a stupid thing to say. Of course she'd worry. He sighed and rubbed a hand over his face. There was only one way either of them would get any sleep.

"Okay, forget that. Come with me."

"Where?"

"Where do you think?" he asked irritably. "It's obvious you won't sleep until you know, so we're going to my office. That's where my computer is."

She touched his arm. "Thank you. Not just for this, but for everything." He shrugged it aside and she said, "I mean it. I don't know why you took me in, or gave me a job, or why you're being so nice, but I appreciate it more than I can say."

"It's not a big deal."

"Yes it is. It's a very big deal, to me."

He shifted uncomfortably and looked away. "I don't want your gratitude."

"No? What do you want, Cam?"

"Not what you're thinking," he said harshly. Which was a big, fat lie and he had a feeling she knew it as well as he did. "I'm not hitting on you," he added, just in case she needed that point clarified.

She smiled. "I know. Rachel told me you didn't hit on your employees."

"That's right." A good rule, a necessary rule. And one he'd never before wished he could break. Until he'd hired Delilah. Without even trying, she was turning everything upside down and sideways. "All I want is for you to do your job. Now, go look this up. You need to get some sleep tonight."

SHE WAS TIRED. So tired. But she had to know for sure. Cam led her to his office and left her with the computer, saying he'd be back later. He didn't make a big deal of it, but she had an idea he didn't like leaving her alone in his office. Which didn't surprise her. After all, he didn't know her any better than she knew him. He'd already trusted her more than she deserved, but he would be stupid not to protect his restaurant. And if she knew one thing, she knew he wasn't stupid.

She started with the obituaries. Nothing. The tightness, the fear, began to ease the longer she searched and found nothing. While she looked, she wondered again why Cam was helping her. He'd made it clear there weren't any strings attached, either. And she believed him.

She'd believed Avery, too. Believed he loved her, believed he'd take care of her. He'd taken care of her all right.

Given that example, she should be more cautious with Cameron. She had been tempted, really tempted to give him Avery's name. To let him share some of the burden. Which was idiotic. She didn't know him. Even if he seemed decent, it didn't mean he really was.

But she didn't have a bad feeling about Cam. Honestly, she thought he was just what he seemed. Of course, she had a history of believing the wrong men, stretching back to when she was sixteen and had unknowingly taken a ride in a car. She'd graduated from trusting a car thief to trusting a killer. Or at the least, an abuser.

Was Cam trustworthy? If he wasn't trustworthy, then he was fooling a lot of people. Unlike Avery, Cam was a public person. Everyone knew him, and as far as she could tell, everyone turned to him. Family, friends, employees. Surely they couldn't all be wrong about the man.

Plus, he lived in a fishbowl. A small town wouldn't be easy to hide in. Unlike a city the size of Houston, where everyone minded their own business.

Why hadn't she seen it with Avery? He'd begun isolating her, but subtly, even before the wedding. He didn't like her friends, never wanted to go out with them. And the wedding, just the two of them at the JP. Avery had said it would be more romantic that way.

She'd rarely met anyone else when she was with him. He'd taken her places, but always alone. Never with either of their friends. He'd weaned her away from her friends, in fact. Which should have set off alarm bells. But she'd wanted to believe him, and she had. Fool that she was.

Finally, she was satisfied that Avery was still alive. But there was something else she needed to research. Something that had driven her to get away from Avery at all costs. If it was true… She typed in a new name and went back to searching.

"How's it going? Any luck?"

She looked up to see Cam standing in the doorway. She had just closed out the search, deleted the history from the computer. She rubbed her neck and sighed. "As far as I can tell, there's nothing about him in the obituaries. And I didn't see any news stories either. I think he's alive."

Which should have been a relief. In a way it was. Much as Avery might deserve it, especially if what she suspected was true, she hadn't wanted to think she'd been responsible for his death. Accidentally or not, she couldn't deal with thinking she'd killed someone.

"Okay, that's good, isn't it? So now you can get some sleep."

She bit her lip as another unwelcome thought came back to her in full force.

"What's wrong now?" He sounded cranky. She couldn't blame him; he was bound to be tired. "He's not dead. Doesn't that set your mind at rest? Now you can forget him."

She wished. "If he's not dead, he'll be looking for me." He'd be furious she left him, furious she'd managed to get away. Beyond his reach, out of his power. She shivered, thinking about what he'd do if he caught up with her.

"You're a long way from Houston. Why would he look for you here? And you're not using your real name, which makes it harder to trace you."

"I know. But it would be just like him to hire someone to find me. Or report me as missing to the police." To his buddies in the department.

She was no young, naive fool. She'd been alone for years now, and a lot of people had tried to take advantage of her. She should have realized what Avery was. Or at least recognized he wasn't what he pretended to be. Why had she fallen for his lies?

Because she'd been lonely. And he'd been very smooth, she had to admit.

Far too smooth to let slip any proof that he'd murdered his first wife. But she didn't know that for sure. Even if a sick feeling in her stomach said it was true, she couldn't prove it.

"After what he did to you, you think he'd go to the cops? Wouldn't he be worried you'd bring charges against him? He locked you up, kept you against your will. That's a crime in anyone's book."

"No, he won't worry. He'll just deny everything. He's a respected—" she halted before she said too much. "He's respected. He's got connections. It's my word against his and guess who will lose in that scenario."

He frowned. "You're forgetting your bruises."

She brushed that aside. "That won't matter." He'd think of a way out of that.

"I know someone on the police force here. Let me take you to her. She'll help."

Too upset to sit still, she got up and paced. "No. I can't risk the police. I just…can't." She'd seen the statistics on battered women. The most dangerous time was when you ran. And if your abuser found you— If she went to the police, he'd find her for sure. Then he would come after her.

And she would die.

Cam got up as well. "Look, we can't do any more tonight. Let's get some sleep and you think about what you want to do. We can talk it over in the morning."

"All right. Is there something you want me to do tomorrow, since the restaurant is closed? Inventory? Laundry?" After all he'd done for her, the least she could do was offer to help on her day off.

"We'll see in the morning. I've got to get up early. I'm supposed to help fix the storm damage on the community center. My brother-in-law Mark conned me into it."

"I shouldn't have kept you up so late," she said, feeling guilty. "Why didn't you say something?"

"It's no big deal. I've gotten by on less sleep. Besides, losing a little sleep is better than having you pacing the floor all night."

They went upstairs. She touched his arm to stop him before he went to his room. His arm was solid, the skin warm. "Thank you."

"You've already thanked me. Several times." He looked annoyed. "You don't need to thank me every ten seconds, Delilah."

"This time I'm thanking you for something different." They stared at each other. Delilah was very aware of him, of his scent, the feel of his arm, so steady, so…comforting. "Thank you for believing me."

She looked at him, at his mouth, conscious of a tingle of awareness, of attraction. What would it be like to kiss him? Would his mouth be soft, hard? Would it be slow? Or fast and reckless? He was staring at her mouth, she realized. Maybe he was thinking about it, too.

"Delilah." His voice was husky. Deep.

"What?"

For a long moment he didn't speak. "Nothing. Get some sleep," he said, and went to his bedroom.

She sucked in an unsteady breath. What was going on? Could she really be falling for a man she'd met only a few days before? Her life was still in turmoil from the last mistake she'd made. And Cam had made it clear he wasn't looking for anything romantic with her. He thought she was too young for him. Way too young, he'd said. She should be glad of his friendship, and stop thinking about the attraction she was finding it harder and harder to deny.

Besides, there was a very good reason she couldn't get involved with Cameron Randolph—she wasn't free of Avery. And since she couldn't let him find her, she wasn't likely to be free of him any time soon. If ever.

CHAPTER FIVE

DELILAH WAS SITTING at the table reading the classified ads when Cam returned from working at the community center the next morning. "How did it go?"

He wore a pair of jeans with one knee ripped out and a short-sleeve T-shirt that had definitely seen better days. "Let's just say I'm glad I'm finished. I hate roofing. Construction is not my thing."

Maybe not, she thought as he opened the refrigerator door and stood with his back to her, but his body looked like he wasn't unfamiliar with physical labor. He had a great set of muscles. All she had to do was close her eyes and remember what his bare chest had looked like. She drew herself up with a start. What was she doing, fantasizing about Cam's bare anything? That was only asking for trouble.

He got a carton of orange juice out of the refrigerator and poured a large glass, then took a seat at the table.

"Want ads or apartments?"

She glanced at him warily. "Neither. I was reading the personals. Do I need to look for a new job?"

"Not as far as I'm concerned."

"And the apartment?"

A corner of his mouth lifted in a smile. "You can stay here as long as you need to."

"Thank you." A good thing, too, since just as Cam had predicted, there was no available housing in Aransas City. She'd been awfully lucky to choose his place to break into. For a number of reasons.

"Have you decided what you're going to do? Are you going to the cops?"

She didn't want to talk about it but knew she had to. "No." She'd thought about it long and hard and decided that going to the police wasn't possible. "I can't do that. If I do that, he could find me. I won't risk it. I'm going to pretend he doesn't exist." And pray he didn't find her and come after her.

Cam seemed about to say something, then shrugged. "All right, if that's what you want."

"You think I'm wrong, don't you?"

"Doesn't matter what I think. It's your decision. I already told you I thought you should tell the cops what the bastard did to you."

"I—can't."

He looked at her for a minute before he nodded. "Okay. Let me know if you change your mind."

"I won't." No, she meant to put Avery Freeman firmly in her past.

He drank some juice. "So, what are you reading? That's the Aransas Bay *Port o' Call*, isn't it?" he asked. The local newspaper covered several of the small towns in the area. Port Aransas, Aransas City, Rockport, Fulton. She wasn't sure what other towns it covered.

"Yes," she said, grateful for the change of subject. She read aloud, "A drunken B. was escorted out of the Neon Moon in Port Aransas. His wife was overheard to say that if he did it again he'd be sleeping in the sand dunes." She looked up at him, laughing. "Is this for real?"

"Oh, yeah." He grinned and drank more. "The *Port o' Call* prints all the gossip from every little town around here. They always use initials, though, and not the right ones, either. But everyone knows who they are. That's about old man Piper. He ties one on about once a month, and his wife always threatens him with the sand dunes."

The *Port o' Call* was about the strangest newspaper she'd ever seen. But then, she was used to big city newspapers. "I've never lived in a small town. It must be interesting."

"It can be. If you like everyone knowing your business, or thinking they do." He drained his juice and got up to take the glass to the sink.

"I need to ask a favor. Where do I get laundry detergent? I used the last of yours and I have to wash." With only one change of clothes, and one of them borrowed, she would be washing daily.

He turned around and looked her up and down, frowning. "You need more clothes. I should have thought of that. I'll take you to buy some and we can go by the grocery store after that. Monday's grocery day anyway."

"Thanks, but I can't afford any more clothes. I'll be fine with what I have."

"I'll lend you the money."

"No. It's nice of you, but I don't want to spend any more than I have to. I need to save, not spend."

He looked annoyed. "I'm not saying you have to buy out the store, but you need some clothes. I don't mind lending you the money."

"I don't—" Frustrated, she started again. "I'm already indebted to you for giving me a job. And a place to stay. I'm not about to take your money for something frivolous when I can't even pay you rent yet."

"Damn it, a couple of shirts and some underwear aren't frivolous."

She said nothing, just set her jaw and looked at him.

"Fine. If you want to be stubborn, have at it. I'm going to take a shower."

He came back a little while later and picked up the keys he'd thrown on the counter. "Let's go."

"Where?" she asked suspiciously.

"Just get in the truck," he told her. "Do you have to argue about every damn thing?"

She didn't think she was being argumentative. She was being practical. If he didn't like that, too bad. Insulted, she followed him down the stairs and out to his truck. Her resolve not to speak lasted until they passed a small grocery store just a few blocks away.

"Is that where you shop?"

"Sometimes." But he didn't stop. Again, they both lapsed into silence. He continued driving until they reached the next town to the south, where he pulled into the parking lot of a discount store.

Delilah stared at him. "Are you deaf? I said I didn't want to borrow money from you."

"I heard you. You're not borrowing from me. I'm giving you the clothes."

"No, absolutely not. I can't accept something like that from you." No way would she go down that road to ruin. She already owed him more than she could repay.

He ground his teeth and frowned at her. "Look, I'm not having one of my employees show up day after day in one of two shirts. It makes it look like I'm not paying you a living wage. Which, while true, isn't anybody's business. So you either go in there and pick up a few shirts and another pair of jeans and some underwear or I'll go in myself and buy them. And knowing women, you won't like what I pick. That's your choice, take it or leave it."

They glared at each other, each unwilling to give in.

After a moment, his expression softened. "Delilah, let me do this. Trust me, it's not a big deal."

"All right," she said finally. "But I'm paying you back." As soon as possible.

"We'll argue about that later."

WHOSE BRILLIANT IDEA was it for him to wait in the lingerie department while Delilah tried on stuff? Cam wondered. He should have waited somewhere else. Anywhere else. Because he couldn't help thinking about what Delilah would look like in some of those skimpy little numbers. He closed his eyes and swore under his breath. Bad idea, thinking about Delilah and underwear. Really bad idea.

"Cam?"

Hearing his name called, he turned around to see

Maggie Barnes, an old friend of his, pushing her cart toward him. Her long red hair was pulled back in a ponytail and her face was bare of makeup, and she wore old jeans and a T-shirt. Still, even dressed like that, she was a pretty woman.

"Hey, Maggie. How's it going?"

"Can't complain." She looked in his cart and raised an eyebrow. "I guess you can't either. New girlfriend?"

"Huh?" He looked down. His cart was filled with an assortment of female items, three pairs of women's panties topping them. He damn near blushed. "No, just waiting on a friend."

She gave him a skeptical glance. "You haven't started cross-dressing, have you?"

He laughed. "No fear of that. I'll stick to men's clothes. Besides—" he gestured at the panties "—they're not my size."

"They do look a little small," she said with a smile.

"Day off?" he asked, since she wasn't wearing her uniform. Maggie had moved away for several years, then about five years ago had returned, apparently for good, and joined the small Aransas City police force.

"No, I'm working the graveyard shift tonight. I had to come get something for Dad before I went in." She rolled her eyes. "He decided he had to have a new cooler for the fish, though why he thinks he needs it now when he can't possibly go out for several more weeks is beyond me."

Maggie's father was a fisherman who'd recently broken his leg, and from what Cam had heard, he'd been running his daughter ragged looking after him.

"How is he doing? He hasn't been in to the restaurant since he hurt his leg."

"He's doing all right, thanks. Just cranky," she said with a laugh.

"Cam, do you know where the—" Delilah stopped beside him, carrying a pair of jeans over her arm. "Sorry, didn't mean to interrupt."

"That's okay. Delilah, this is Maggie Barnes. Maggie, Delilah Roberts." They nodded at each other and Cam added, "Delilah's new in town. She's working at the restaurant."

Maggie looked at the cart, then gave Delilah a slow perusal, finally turning back to Cam. "Definitely not cross-dressing." Then she whispered, "A little young, isn't she?"

"Maggie—" he started to say something else, but then he shrugged and didn't. He wasn't going to explain that he and Delilah didn't have anything going, like Maggie clearly thought. For one thing, it was none of her business.

Maggie ignored him and turned to Delilah. "How are you liking Aransas City?"

"It's a nice town," Delilah said.

"Plan on staying long?"

"I'm not sure," Delilah said and glanced at Cam.

"I imagine Cam will have something to say about that. Well, I gotta get going. See you around, Cam. Nice to meet you," she said to Delilah and walked off.

"What did she mean, you'd have something to say about how long I stay in town? Why did she say that?" Delilah asked him.

He picked up a pair of panties from the cart and dangled them from his fingers. "Probably because of these."

"Sorry. It's your fault, though. You were the one who insisted I buy clothes."

"That's right. Because you needed them."

"Well, it's your problem, not mine. But I expect you can handle your girlfriends. According to gossip, you don't have a problem with that."

Cam wondered what she'd heard. No telling what Martha and Rachel had told her. "Maggie's not my girlfriend. She's an old friend of mine."

"I got the feeling she was more than that."

Cam shook his head. He saw no reason to explain they'd once been involved. The physical part of their relationship was over a long time ago.

"Maybe she'd like to be."

He laughed. "Trust me, she wouldn't."

Delilah glanced down the aisle, the way Maggie had gone. "She's a cop, isn't she?"

"Yeah. How did you know that?"

"It's in the eyes. I've been looked at just like that by too many cops not to recognize it when I see it."

"I thought you said you weren't in trouble with the law?"

"I'm not. That doesn't mean I haven't ever had a run-in with them." When he didn't speak, she added, "I've seen a lot of cops. I've been on my own since I was sixteen."

Which was why she seemed older than she was, he decided. "You're imagining things with Maggie. I didn't notice her acting weird."

"That's because you're a man."

He grinned. "Yeah, last time I checked I was." And unfortunately for him, Delilah was all woman.

GROCERY SHOPPING in Aransas City was an interesting and time-consuming experience, especially with Cam. He knew everyone, and they all wanted to stop and chat. After the fifth person had stopped them, she asked, "How do you ever get anything done? What if you're in a hurry?"

He smiled and picked up a head of lettuce.

"Doesn't pay to be in a hurry in Aransas City. Nobody here knows the meaning of the word, so you just might as well relax."

"It does seem to have a slower pace. Have you lived here all your life?"

"Most of it." He picked some apples, then pushed the cart down the aisle. "I was in the service for a couple of years and after boot camp, I lived in Germany. After that I went to college at the University of Texas at Austin, but other than that I've been here."

"You went to college?" She knew she sounded wistful. Hell, she was wistful.

He grinned. "For a couple of years, but it wasn't really my thing. Then I heard the Scarlet Parrot was for sale, so I left and came back here. Been here ever since."

"I went to college for a couple of years," she admitted. She'd been in school part-time when she'd met Avery. After they married he had forced her to quit. "I wish I'd finished."

"Why didn't you?"

She frowned, wishing she hadn't said anything. "It just…didn't work out."

He looked at her searchingly. "You could go back."

"I don't have the money now."

"You can go part-time. There are lots of community colleges around that aren't too expensive."

"Maybe I will." If she ever felt secure enough to spend money on school. Secure enough not to worry that somehow Avery would find her.

He stopped on the aisle with detergents. "What kind do you like?"

"I usually get whatever is cheapest."

He turned his back and reached for one on the top shelf.

A woman with a baby in her cart and holding a young boy's hand stopped beside them. "Cam, just the person I've been looking for."

He turned around and looked at her. "Whatever it is, no." He put the detergent in the cart.

"Very funny. You have to at least listen before you say no."

The child, a dark-haired boy of about four, had been pulling on Cam's pants leg insistently. Cam smiled at him and ruffled his hair. "Hey, Max."

"Up," he demanded, raising his arms.

Cam obligingly picked him up and settled him on his hip. The little boy immediately started talking but Delilah couldn't understand what he said since both adults were talking, too. Then the baby chimed in and she couldn't comprehend a thing.

After a couple of minutes of the din, Cam spoke

to the boy. "Max, if you're quiet while your mom and I talk, she'll buy you a piece of candy."

Max immediately shut his mouth.

"I'll buy him candy? You should have to, not me. Besides, you shouldn't bribe him," the woman said. "You always do that and it's a terrible example."

"Worked, didn't it?" He put Max down and got the little girl out of the cart. She had curly dark hair and big brown eyes and was gazing adoringly at Cam. "Hello, Miranda. You get prettier every day," he said and gave her a smacking kiss on the cheek that had her giggling.

"You must be Delilah," the woman said. "I'm Cam's sister, Cat."

"Nice to meet you," she said. Unlike his other sister, this one didn't look like him. But she did see a resemblance to their brother Gabe. Gabe, who she still didn't feel comfortable around. She didn't think he liked her if that little bit of conversation she'd overheard was any indication.

"What do you want, Cat?" Cam put the baby back in the cart and buckled her in. "I'd like to get home sometime today and I still have shopping to do."

"Well, don't bite my head off. I want you to come to dinner tonight." She turned to Delilah. "We'd love for you to come, too, Delilah."

To say she was shocked was putting it mildly. "Oh, thanks, but—"

Cat interrupted her before she could gracefully decline. "I won't take no for an answer. From either of you. Seven o'clock. The kids go to bed at seven-thirty, so it will only be chaotic for a short time," she said, for Delilah's benefit.

"Your house, not chaotic? Now that's a laugh," Cam said. "There's always chaos at your house. You and Mark never have anything but chaos. Unless it's pandemonium."

Cat gave him a dirty look but didn't deny it. "Chicken parmigiana," she said. "And if you're not rude to me, I'll make crème brûlée for dessert."

"Crème brûlée? You know that's my favorite."

With a smug smile, she said, "I know. So, I'll see you both at seven. Don't be late." Apparently feeling that clinched the matter, she walked off.

"Candy," Delilah heard Max say. "Want candy."

"We'll pick some out at the counter," his mother said.

"I'm sorry," Delilah said, watching them leave. "You don't need to take me to dinner. I'm sure your sister was just being polite."

He snorted. "You don't know Cat. She's not polite, she's nosy."

"About me?"

"About you and me," he clarified. "But don't worry, I'll set her straight. And you won't mind going to dinner. Cat's annoying sometimes, but she's a great cook."

"I'd love to go." She shouldn't. She had no business going out with him.

It's just a family dinner, she thought. Not a date. Surely she could do that. Be with a normal man. Platonically. A man she wouldn't have to worry would turn into a monster. A man who liked children and lived in the midst of a big family. She wanted to know him better. She wished…it didn't matter what she wished. At least she had Cam's friendship. Anything else was impossible, for too many reasons to count.

THAT AFTERNOON after he'd run his errands, Cam decided to stock the bar. He was headed downstairs when Gabe came in. "Just the man I wanted to see. I could use some help bringing some stock up."

"I'll do it for a cold one," Gabe said.

"You're on."

A short time later Cam was opening boxes and stowing the beer and liquor while Gabe sipped a cold brew.

"So, where's the hot chick?" Gabe asked, glancing around.

"If you mean Delilah, she's in her room. Why?"

"Just curious." He took another sip of beer. "Did you ever check her references?"

"No." He hadn't asked her because he knew she wouldn't have given them to him. Just as she hadn't shared the bastard's name who had beaten her up. "What's this obsession you have with Delilah?"

He rolled a shoulder. "It's not an obsession. I think you need to be more careful. I've got a feeling about her."

Cam ducked down below to line up liquor bottles. When he came up he said, "You've got a feeling because she turned you down."

"That's not it."

"Sure it isn't."

"Cam."

He sounded serious, something rare with Gabe. Cam glanced at his brother, waited for him to continue.

"She reminds me of someone. A woman who was really bad news."

Cam knew most of the women Gabe had dated and he couldn't imagine who he was talking about. Although, there had been a period of Gabe's life that he was still secretive about. When he'd had the gambling problem that had nearly cost him his business. "Someone you were involved with," he said.

Gabe hesitated, then nodded. "A long time ago. But you don't forget."

"I know. Believe me, I haven't forgotten Janine," he said, referring to his ex-fiancée. "But I don't see what any of this has to do with Delilah working here."

"As long as she's just working, nothing. But if you're sleeping with her—"

"What is with you? What are you so worried about? You think I'm going to fall madly in love and give her all my worldly goods?"

"No, but I think you're madly in lust and that tends to make a guy stupid. Have you slept with her yet?"

"Why this sudden interest in my sex life?"

"You have."

"No, I haven't and I don't plan on it. She's working for me and living here. You know I don't date my help. Or sleep with them."

"None of your other help looks like Delilah." Gabe got up and came around the bar to put his beer bottle in the trash. He looked at Cam. "I never said anything to you about Janine. I should have."

"What about her?"

"I knew Janine was cheating on you."

Surprised, he stared at Gabe. "You knew and you didn't tell me? Why the hell did you keep quiet?"

"Okay, I didn't *know* exactly." He squeezed the bridge of his nose. "Let's just say I wasn't surprised when you caught her in the sack with Travis."

Light dawned. "She came on to you."

Gabe nodded. "I have to tell you, if you hadn't been my brother I'd have taken her up on the offer in a heartbeat. That was one seriously hot chick."

"Delilah's not Janine."

"No, but she might be worse."

"Gabe, give it a rest. You don't have to worry." Cam was doing enough thinking for both of them. Because no matter how many times he told himself he wasn't going to bed with Delilah, there were just as many times when he knew he wanted to, and in other circumstances, he would have. Or he'd have tried like hell to make sure it did happen.

CHAPTER SIX

THE ONLY THING DIFFERENT about dinner at his sister's house that night was Delilah's presence. That was a big difference, though, since Cam never took women to any family affair. Unless his mother had a party and he needed a date, and then he never took the same woman twice. It was a form of self-defense he'd perfected over the years.

Dinner at Cat's wasn't the same as a big party at his mother's house in Key Allegro. Those were usually sophisticated affairs she dragged her children to by dint of threats and coercion. Sophisticated wasn't what anyone would think of in connection with a meal at Mark and Cat's.

When they got there, Mark met them at the door. He said hi to Delilah, thrust a squalling, furious baby into Cam's arms and disappeared, after shouting at Cat that their company had arrived. Cat, naturally, was nowhere to be seen.

Cam looked at Delilah over Miranda's head and grinned. "What did I tell you?"

"Is it always like this?"

"Unless the kids are asleep." He cuddled Miranda in the crook of his arm. "Isn't that right, sweetheart?" he said, and tickled her chin until she stopped crying.

A raucous caw came from the living room as they walked in. "Hello, sucker," Buddy, his sister's African gray parrot screeched.

Delilah looked startled, then laughed when she spotted the bird. She walked over to his cage. "Well, hello there. Aren't you pretty? What's your name?"

"Buddy," Cam said, smiling at the bird now flirting with Delilah. "That's one of the milder things he says. Cat's been working on him since she doesn't want the kids to repeat some of his worst comments. He's a lot better than he used to be, which is a good thing since it would kill her to have to give him away."

"Pretty girl," Buddy said to Delilah adoringly.

She looked at Cam and smiled. "I think he likes me."

"Sounds like it." Cam didn't tell her Buddy liked almost all women. He put Miranda up on his shoulder and patted her back. She wore her pajamas and smelled clean, as only a freshly bathed baby can.

"Looks like you're sleepy, princess," he said when she snuggled her face into his neck.

Delilah was looking at him with a curious expression. "What?" he asked. "Did she spit up on my shoulder?" He turned his head to look, but luckily, she hadn't.

Delilah shook her head. "No, it's— You look so natural holding her."

He laughed. "I should. I've had lots of practice. Gail has three kids and Cat has two."

"Have you ever thought about having your own kids?"

"Nope," he said, but that was a lie. "I'd have to be married and that's not happening." Which wasn't a lie. When he'd been engaged to Janine, he'd thought about having kids. Someday. But when they'd broken up, he'd quit thinking about having a family of his own.

Delilah didn't look as if she believed him, but she didn't comment.

Cat came in just then and took Miranda from him. "Hi, Delilah. Sorry about this. I'll go put Miranda down. Cam, get Delilah something to drink. Mark and I will be back in a minute."

"That's an optimistic estimate," Cam told Delilah. "What can I get you?"

"Whatever you're having is fine." She followed him into the kitchen.

He pulled out a couple of beers from the refrigerator. "There's some white zinfandel wine in here if you'd rather have that."

"No, beer's good." She looked around the kitchen and sniffed the air. "That smells wonderful. Like being at an Italian restaurant. It was awfully nice of your sister to ask me to dinner."

He started to comment but Max came barreling through the door screeching, "Uncle Cam", at the top of his lungs. He flung himself at Cam, clutching his leg.

"Daddy's mad at me."

Max wore his best abused air, but since Cam knew Mark had never lifted a finger to the child, he wasn't taken in. Cam picked him up, noticing he was ready for bed, too. "What did you do this time, big guy?"

Max grinned, a dimple winking in his cheek. Mark entered the room, looking harried. Cam didn't blame him, Max was a hellion. A great kid, but a hellion.

"He flushed a toy truck down the toilet," Mark said. "So don't go in the hall bathroom unless you want to wade through a flood. You'll have to use mine and Cat's." He turned to Delilah. "Welcome to the madhouse. I'm Mark, by the way. I don't think I had a chance to introduce myself when you first came in."

"Delilah," she said and shook hands with him. "Thank you for having me."

"Glad you could come. I'll go put Max to bed and then hopefully we can eat." He took the boy from Cam. "Come on, son."

Max put his arms around Mark's neck and hugged him exuberantly. "Are you still mad at me, Daddy?" Max asked as his father carried him away.

"No, Max," Cam heard Mark say. "But don't flush any more toys, okay?"

"It amazes me how Max and Miranda have him wrapped around their fingers. He busts animal smugglers, but with those kids he's putty."

"I think it's sweet," Delilah said. "They're so…normal."

He thought that was kind of an odd comment. "As opposed to abnormal?"

She looked at him as if she'd forgotten he was there. "Your sister and brother-in-law are nice. That's all I meant." She went into the living room and he heard her talking to the bird.

Delilah and Cat hit it off right away, which was a mixed blessing. Cat would be sure to go into full matchmaking mode. But she'd have done that anyway. As would Gail. In fact, Gabe was the only one of his siblings who seemed to have issues with Delilah. But since Cam didn't intend for anything to happen, what his family thought of Delilah didn't really matter.

After dinner, Delilah took her dishes to the kitchen. "Let me help you wash up," she said to Cat, who was already at the sink.

"Oh, no you don't. That's Cam's job. It's the least he can do."

So Delilah went off with Mark to see the birds in the aviary. And Cam, just as his sister had planned, was left alone with Cat. Cam had been expecting this all evening. Ever since Cat had married Mark, she had wanted him and Gabe to settle down, too. She refused to believe he just wasn't interested.

"Delilah seems nice." She shot Cam a speculative glance. "And she's very pretty." He nodded but didn't say anything. "She's smart, too."

He picked up a pan to dry it. "Why do you say that?" He knew Delilah was very bright but he wanted to know why Cat thought so.

"When we were talking about accounting it became fairly obvious. Did you know she wanted to be a CPA before she said it tonight at dinner?"

"No." Cat was a CPA as well as a bird rehabber. As a Fish and Wildlife Service special agent, Mark was interested in the birds, but accounting wasn't his thing any more than it was Cam's. Cam figured Cat had been in heaven to have someone to talk accounting with.

"She said she'd gone to a couple of years of college, but she didn't say what she'd studied." He'd seen Cat and Delilah with their heads together but he hadn't heard all of the conversation since he'd been talking to Mark at the time. "So, did you talk her into going back to school?"

"No. I offered to lend her some books but she wouldn't take them. Said she'd go to the library. Why wouldn't she let me lend them to her, do you know?"

"I'm not sure. She doesn't like to owe anybody." As he picked up another dish, he thought about the shopping trip and the fit she'd pitched about borrowing money from him. "Maybe she thinks she won't be in town that long."

Cat looked surprised. "Why would she leave? Especially since you and she—"

"Let me save you some trouble," he interrupted. "Nothing's going on. And nothing's going to go on. So you can forget about it."

She scrubbed on another pan, her dark hair falling forward to shield her face. "Why not?"

"What do you mean why not? It's obvious."

"Not to me. Why not?" she repeated, tilting her head to look at him. "Mark thinks you have the hots for her. And it's pretty clear she doesn't dislike you. So, what's the problem?"

He ground his teeth. Damn his nosy family. "Mark needs to keep his mouth shut. And you need to butt out."

Cat looked at him and laughed. "Oh, yeah, that's going to happen. Come on, Cam. Tell me the problem."

He put the dish down on the drain board. "Cat, she's fifteen years younger than me."

"Really?" She stopped scrubbing and looked at him. "She sure doesn't seem that young."

"Yeah, well, she is." But Cat was right, she seemed older. She was a woman, not a girl.

"I still don't get it. What's the big deal about you being older than her?" When he didn't answer she continued, "Is this about Janine?"

"No, it's not about Janine." His ex-fiancée had absolutely nothing to do with his feelings about Delilah. Damn it, now he was having to admit he did have feelings about her. But he wouldn't admit it to Cat.

"Good. Because it's really time you got over that. She is so not worth it."

"I am over it. One has nothing to do with the other." He set a pot down and sighed. "Delilah is living with me and working for me. Nothing's going to happen." Because once he had Delilah, he wasn't so sure he could walk away, like he did with other women. And he didn't do any other kind of relationship.

"I still don't see why you—"

He interrupted her, throwing his towel down on the counter. "Damn it, Cat, drop it. Nothing is going to happen between Delilah and me. Got it?"

"I think we all got it," Mark said. He was standing in the doorway with Delilah just behind him.

"Well, shit," Cam muttered. What had started out a nice evening was going downhill fast.

"I HAD A GREAT TIME," Delilah said on the way home. "I really liked your sister and brother-in-law." She'd almost forgotten what it was like to go out, Avery had prevented that for so long. She shook her head, determined not to think about him tonight.

"They liked you, too. Which reminds me, why wouldn't you let Cat lend you some books? If you're really interested in accounting, she could help you out."

"It was sweet of her to offer. But there's not much point in it. I can't afford to go back to school right now." If she could have afforded it…if she could know that she'd be around to enroll… But she couldn't be sure of either of those things.

"You should check into it before you say that.

Some of the community colleges are surprisingly affordable."

"I can't even afford rent yet. How am I supposed to go to school?"

"Would you quit worrying about rent? Have I asked you to pay me rent?"

"No, but you should."

"Why?" They reached the restaurant and he put the truck in park and turned in his seat to look at her. "I don't need the money. And you do."

"Why are you being so nice to me? At first I thought you might—" She broke off, unwilling to say what she'd thought. Besides, seduction clearly hadn't been on his agenda. She should be glad about that, and she was. Still, she was feminine enough to feel a little irritation that he was so adamant about not getting involved with her.

Cam finished the sentence for her. "You thought I'd let you stay with me so I could make a move on you."

She looked down at her clasped hands. "Yes."

"Delilah, look at me." He waited until she did to continue. "You know I wouldn't do that, don't you?"

"If I didn't, you made it clear tonight in your sister's kitchen." Again, she felt that spurt of annoyance. Maybe he didn't find her attractive.

"I told you, my sister is nosy. I was just setting her straight."

He got out of the truck and so did she. She waited until they went upstairs to the apartment before she spoke again. "Can I ask you something?"

"Sure. What?"

"Why are you so sure nothing's going to happen between you and me?"

He halted in the act of removing his jacket and looked at her. "What?"

"Why is nothing going to happen between us?"

He finished taking off his jacket and hung it on the coatrack. "You know why."

"Because you're not attracted to me." She should shut up, now, but her mouth took on a life of its own.

"I didn't say that." He swore beneath his breath. "You're my employee and you're living here. Not to mention, I'm fifteen years older than you. The two of us getting involved wouldn't be a good idea. I figured you agreed with me about that. Don't you?"

She looked away, then nodded. "You're right. I'm sorry I—I'm sorry. Forget I said anything."

What was wrong with her? She had no right thinking about Cam in any other way than friendship.

But he wasn't indifferent to her.

And she sure as hell wasn't indifferent to him.

CHAPTER SEVEN

CAM WAS HAVING a damned hard time keeping his hands to himself and off Delilah. Since that night at Cat's, it had been getting harder. She'd agreed they were better off not becoming involved. He knew she'd been tempted. Why else would she have asked him what she had? But Delilah was young and vulnerable. He couldn't take advantage of her. That didn't stop him from thinking about her, though.

He stumbled to the shower one morning and stopped as Delilah came out of the bathroom with a towel wrapped around her. Her smooth, shapely shoulders gleamed above the white terry cloth. Her dark hair was wet and slicked back from her face. His gaze fell from her face to her chest and he saw drops of moisture disappearing into her cleavage. He wanted to trace the moisture with his tongue, flick open that towel and see her beautiful body, touch and caress every inch of her soft, creamy, fragrant skin.

He raised his gaze and met her eyes. She smiled and said something but he couldn't hear it over the roar of blood rushing to his head. Not to mention the blood rushing to other places. He mumbled a curse, pushed past her and closed the bathroom door, sucked in a deep breath, thinking he was safe.

The room was warm, steamy. It smelled like Delilah, like the scent of roses from the body wash she used. Then he saw her underwear, red thong panties, hanging over the shower rod. He reached for them, to move them so they wouldn't get wetter. Held them in his hands and thought about sliding them down her legs, inch by luscious inch. Closing his eyes, he gritted his teeth and thought about banging his head against the wall, but he didn't believe it would do any good.

He needed a woman.

The frigid shower he took only made him cold. It didn't do a thing to take care of his other problem. He'd known it almost from the first. Living with Delilah and not having her was going to kill him.

Twenty minutes later, he'd managed to get himself under control. So what if he was irritable as hell? He'd live through it. He was reading the paper when he heard a knock on his kitchen door. He got up to let Maggie in, wondering what she wanted.

Her hair was loose and fell to her shoulders in rich cinnamon waves. He often forgot how pretty it was because she usually wore it scraped back in a pony-tail.

"Hey, Maggie. What's going on?"

"Not much. I just thought I'd stop by before you open up for lunch. Hadn't talked to you in a while. Got any more coffee?"

"Sure." He got a mug down, filled it and gave it to her. He thought her explanation a little odd, since he'd seen her a few days before, but he didn't say anything.

"Where's your new friend?" she said, after taking a sip of coffee.

"Down in the restaurant, setting up. Why?"

"No reason." She took a drink of her coffee and sighed with pleasure. "You always did make great coffee."

She seemed funny. Different, somehow. He couldn't put his finger on it, then realized what it was. "You're wearing makeup."

"Yeah. So?"

"And you're dressed up." She was wearing slacks and a nice shirt—one that clung to the curves he usually forgot she had—instead of her usual jeans and T-shirt. "I get it. Hot date later?"

She flushed and he knew he was on to something.

"Can't a woman wear something decent once in a while without having a date?"

"Sure, but you never do."

"I felt like wearing something different, okay? Is that a damn crime?"

He spread his hands in a peacemaking gesture. "Hey, just an observation. No need to bite my head off."

She hunched a shoulder and fell silent. By now she'd really gotten his curiosity up, but he knew better than to rush her. Maggie would get to her point when she was good and ready, not before. He went back to reading the paper, secure that she'd eventually say what was on her mind.

"You've really got the town buzzing."

He glanced up. "Why is that?"

"Come on, Cam." She lifted an eyebrow. "Delilah, of course. You can't let a woman that pretty live with you and expect people not to talk. Especially when you haven't ever had a woman living with you before."

"Who I let live with me is my business."

"Doesn't stop people from talking."

He grunted and looked away. He couldn't have said why it bothered him, except it irritated him that people were gossiping about something that wasn't even happening.

Maybe it irritated him so much *because* there was nothing happening.

"So, are you serious about this girl?"

He stared at her, wondering where she was coming from. But since it was Maggie and he'd been friends with her for a long time, he answered. "Hell, no, I'm not serious. I'm not even sleeping with her. I'm just helping her out."

"If you say so."

He gave a snort and got up to refill his coffee mug.

"Can you get off work early tonight?"

He turned around and looked at her. "I don't know. Depends on Martha. Why?"

"I've got the night off. I thought maybe you could come over and we could…hang out. I can make burgers or something."

"You're offering to cook for me? Now I know something weird is going on." Maggie didn't cook. She survived on her mother's cooking, restaurant or fast food and, in a pinch, rice.

She got up and walked over to him. Ran her hand lightly up his arm. "I don't have to cook. We could do…other things."

She said it with a smile that looked—wow, if he hadn't known better he'd have thought she was coming on to him.

"Like what?"

"Use your imagination," she told him, sliding her hand over to his shoulder.

Okay, that smile was definitely seductive. This was getting weirder and weirder. And making him…nervous, for God's sake. This wasn't the Maggie he was used to.

"What's going on, Maggie?"

She laughed. "Sometimes you're really dense, Cam." She leaned in and kissed him. And not a friendly peck like they gave each other once in a while. No, this was the real deal, tongues and all. She kissed him like she hadn't kissed him in twelve years. It shocked the hell out of him, to the point that he just stood there, his mind blank.

She finally drew back and smiled at him.

He stared at her a long moment before he found his voice. "What was that?"

Her smile faded. "I'd say that's pretty obvious."

"But you—but we—we decided a long time ago we were better friends than lovers."

"No, Cam, you decided that. You were so busted up over Janine you didn't ask me what I wanted."

He shoved a hand through his hair and paced away from her. "You'd just broken up with someone. You wouldn't tell me his name, but you told me that. You didn't know what you were doing any more than I did." He'd felt bad about it, and a little guilty, because he'd always felt like he'd taken advantage of her. Which was one of the reasons their fling hadn't lasted long.

"I knew exactly what I was doing. I wanted you then. And I want you now. But you've made it pretty clear you don't feel the same."

He didn't want to hurt her. And she was hurting, that was plain. But it didn't make sense. "Why now? Why not five years ago, when you moved back to town? What happened to make you decide you wanted us to get together again?" Because he didn't believe she'd been mooning over him for the last twelve years.

She scowled at him, then shrugged. "I'm tired of being alone, all right? I'm sick and tired of going to bed alone, night after night. I wanted to be with someone, to be close to a man again."

"Are you telling me you haven't had sex since we—"

"Of course I have," she said, interrupting him. "But it's been a long time. And I—I trust you, Cam."

At least she hadn't said she loved him. She was lonely, that was all. He went to her, grasped her arms, rubbed his hands gently up and down them. "You know I care about you, Maggie. But I can't. It wouldn't be right. You deserve someone who loves you. Not just a good time in the sack with a friend."

"I don't see anybody lining up for the job."

"You will." He touched her cheek and smiled. "You're an awesome woman, Maggie."

"Right. If I'm so great why won't you go to bed with me? You don't seem to have a problem bedding other women." Unsmiling, she searched his eyes. "It's because of her, isn't it? You turned me down because of Delilah."

Oh, crap. His hand fell away from her face. It was true, he realized. At least partially. "I told you I wasn't sleeping with her."

"But you want to."

He didn't deny it. What was the point? "This has nothing to do with Delilah. It's between you and me. I'm not going to let you do something you'd regret five minutes after it happened."

"Well, well. Aren't you all fine and noble," she drawled.

"I'm not being noble. I'm trying to make sure you don't get hurt. Maggie—" He grabbed her arm again as she started to move away.

"Oh, save it."

"Cam, Rachel called—" Delilah halted in the doorway. "Sorry, I didn't realize you had company."

"Perfect," Maggie said with disgust and jerked away from him. Propping her hands on her hips, she aimed a look at him that made him feel like the lowest slime alive. "I'll tell you what, Cam. You can take all your precious nobility and stuff it where the sun don't shine." She strode to the back door, yanked it open and slammed it behind her.

"Ouch," Delilah said.

He swore, a single word he didn't normally say around a woman. "How much of that did you hear?" he asked Delilah.

"Just her parting shot. She looked really pissed."

"No kidding."

"Want to talk about it?" she asked sympathetically.

Cam laughed shortly. "No." He scrubbed his hands over his face. There wasn't anything he could do. Either Maggie would get over it or she wouldn't. "What did you want?" he asked Delilah.

"Rachel called and said she'd be late. Something about a project that's due."

"Great. She'd better not be lying or I swear I'm going to fire her."

"You wouldn't."

"Don't count on it." The mood he was in now, he could do it in a heartbeat.

"It's not her fault your shorts are in a twist over whatever happened with you and Maggie."

He opened his mouth to say something rude, then shut it. She had a point. And it wasn't Delilah's fault either. Not about Maggie and not about the fact that he couldn't have what he wanted. Who he wanted.

The knowledge of that didn't improve his temper. So he left the room before he said, or did, something he'd regret later.

"THE LAUNDRY CALLED and said their delivery truck was broken," Delilah told him a few days later.

He looked up at her and frowned. Not wanting a repeat of the shower scene—the one that had been replaying in his head nearly every moment of the last few days—Cam had gotten up early, showered, and gone down to his office to get some hated paperwork done.

"We don't have enough linens for the lunch crowd. Do you want to go get it?"

No. He had a number of other things he needed to do and picking up laundry was nowhere on his list. "This is the sixth time this month their truck has broken down. I should find a new laundry."

"Why don't you?"

Reasonable question. He knew what would be best for his business, unfortunately it wouldn't be best for the laundry. "I would if dropping them wouldn't put them out of business. I've known the owner my entire life. That's the problem with little towns." He ran a hand through his hair. "Can you drive a stick shift?"

"Yes. Why?"

"Take my truck and go pick it up. A-1 Laundry. It's on Redbird Lane, just off Main Street. You can't miss it." She didn't say anything, she just stared at him. "What? You're not a bad driver, are you?"

"No, I'm a good driver. It's just— You're trusting me to take your truck?"

"Shouldn't I? You're not going to wreck it, are you?" He didn't stop to analyze why he was trusting her when he didn't normally—okay, ever—let anyone drive his truck. Especially women.

"Not on purpose," she said. "But accidents happen."

"Just be careful. And hurry up. The lunch crowd will be here before long."

And there was the added bonus that once Delilah left, he would be able to get some work done instead of staring at her and thinking about what would have happened if he'd taken that damn towel off her.

DELILAH HAD MADE IT to the laundry, picked up the restaurant's order and was headed back when she heard the sound of a siren coming up behind her. She glanced in the rearview mirror and saw flashing red and blue lights. Cops. Wonderful. She pulled over and waited. She hated getting pulled over. It made her feel sixteen, helpless, and stupid, all over again.

"Now what? I know I wasn't speeding," she said, watching the officer get out of the prowler. Great, just her luck. Maggie Barnes came up to the window.

She looked nothing like she had the last time Delilah had seen her. Wearing her crisp navy uniform, her clunky cop shoes, and with mirrored dark glasses covering her eyes, she looked every inch the cop she was.

"Officer Barnes, hi. I wasn't speeding, was I?"

"Ms. Roberts." She nodded. "No, not speeding. Can I see your license and registration?"

Her license. The one with a different name than the one she was going by now. If Maggie Barnes ran it through the system that license could lead Avery right to her. "I don't have my license with me," she lied.

Maggie said nothing but Delilah could feel that sharp gaze lasering in on her from behind the dark shades.

"In fact, I, uh, I lost it."

"You lost it." Her tone held no inflection.

Delilah resisted squirming, barely. "I know I shouldn't be driving without it, but I was just running to the cleaners for Cam."

"Uh-huh. What about the registration?"

She looked in the glove compartment. At least that was where it was supposed to be, she thought and pulled it out.

"This isn't my truck. It's Cam's." Which, of course, she'd know. But Delilah felt compelled to say something to break the awkward silence.

Maggie was writing down the information from the registration onto a paper on her clipboard. "I'm aware of that. That's why I pulled you over. Does Cam know you're driving his truck?"

"Of course he does. Why else would I have it?"

She looked up, and Delilah didn't need to see those eyes to read the distrust in them. "That's what I want to know. Cam never lets anyone drive his truck. Especially not women."

Her stomach sank. "Well, he let me. He asked me to go to the laundry for him. Their truck broke and he needed the linens for the restaurant."

Maggie Barnes still didn't say anything. She just stood there, her skepticism patent.

Her irritation getting the best of her, Delilah snapped, "Look in the back if you don't believe me."

"Thanks, I will." She glanced at the back seat where the neat pile of plastic-covered linens sat. "Looks like laundry, all right."

She pulled her glasses off and stuck them in her pocket. Pinned Delilah with the cop look common to every police officer she'd ever run into. And since the age of sixteen, she'd run into a lot of them.

"Sure you want to stick to that story?" Maggie looked at her with unfriendly eyes.

Anger clawed at her but she held it back. "Why don't you ask Cam? I doubt you'll believe anything I say."

"Oh, don't worry, Ms. Roberts, I will. You do know grand theft auto is a felony?"

"I didn't steal Cam's truck." *Wouldn't that be ironic?* she thought. She hadn't stolen a car before, either, but that hadn't saved her from being arrested. Still, she wasn't really worried about getting thrown in jail for auto theft. She didn't want a cop digging around in her background. Avery had too many connections with the Houston police for her to feel safe with any kind of official inquiry. Which was why she'd refused to give her license. But one look at Maggie Barnes's grim face assured her the lady wouldn't be cutting Delilah any breaks any time soon.

"You'd best hope not." She went to her car and talked on the radio, then came back to the truck and pulled out a cell phone. "We'll just give Cam a call and see what he has to say about all this."

She's just doing her job, and looking out for a friend of hers, Delilah thought, struggling with her temper. Watching her, she knew there was more to it. Maggie Barnes didn't much like her, and Delilah had a hunch she knew why. Especially after walking in on that little scene between Cam and his good friend Maggie the other morning.

"Cam, it's Maggie. I've got Delilah Roberts pulled over. Did you know she was driving your pickup? Claims you gave her permission." She glanced at Delilah as she listened. "All right," she said after a minute. "What the hell did you expect me to do? I'm a cop, remember? I thought she'd stolen it. You never let anyone drive your truck."

She frowned at Delilah as she listened some more. "She may not have boosted your truck, but she's driving without a license. I could take her in for that." She paused again. "I don't care if you saw it, I haven't seen it."

She turned her back and walked away but Delilah could still hear her. "No, I don't have to, but I should. I've got a feeling this girl's not on the up-and-up. Are you sure you know what you're doing, Cam?"

Finally, she hung up and came back to the truck. "He asked me not to take you in. Which by all rights, I should do. But since Cam asked me, I'll let you go with a warning. Don't let me catch you driving without your license again, because none of Cam's sweet talk will save you next time. Understand?"

"I understand." Delilah clenched her jaw hard to keep from saying anything else. She wanted to say something rude so badly she could taste it. But if she'd learned anything since her mother died, it was not to smart off to a cop. It tended to piss them off, and once that happened, being run in was inevitable.

So she said nothing. She drove off carefully, making sure she obeyed the speed limit all the way back to the restaurant. By the time she got there, some of her anger had faded and fear had set in.

CHAPTER EIGHT

CAM EXPECTED DELILAH to come see him when she got back from the laundry and was a little surprised when she didn't show. So he went looking for her. He found her in her bedroom, sitting on her bed and stuffing things into her backpack. "What are you doing?"

"Leaving."

"I can see that. Why?"

She flashed him an angry glance. "Because I can't afford to stick around while your girlfriend runs me through the system."

"I told you, Maggie's not my girlfriend. And since you didn't give her your license, I don't see how she'll run you."

"She'll be over here asking you for my social security number or something. Which you don't have and she'll want to know why. I don't think she's going to let this go. She doesn't like me, and I know why."

He crossed the room and sat beside her on the bed. "You are way overreacting. Nothing happened."

She stared at him. "Overreacting? Your *friend* thought I'd stolen your truck. She wanted to take me to jail and throw away the key. And the worst of it was, I couldn't say a word because if I had, she would have done it."

"No, she wouldn't. Not without cause. And not after she talked to me." Maggie was a fair person, and a good cop. But Delilah didn't look like she was buying that. "Maggie was just doing her job. It didn't occur to me she would stop you. It should have, but it didn't. So if you're upset, blame me, not her."

"It doesn't matter who's to blame. What matters is that I can't afford to do anything that might lead A—might lead him to me. Don't you get it?"

"I get that you're terrified of this guy. But he's the one who should be worried. It doesn't make sense to me that if you're so scared of him you won't go to the cops. Why don't you just tell them what he did to you and let them handle it? Assault and kidnapping are pretty serious charges. Maybe he's cut his losses and written you off."

"He won't do that. You don't understand."

"No, I don't. But I understand that you can't keep

running. You don't have the resources. At least here you've got a job. And a place to stay."

She fiddled with her backpack, then looked up at him. "Why do you want me to stay?" She said it quietly with a hint of huskiness in her voice.

It surprised him how badly he wanted to comfort her. To touch her, hold her. "I want to help you." He wanted a lot more than that, but he wasn't going to say it. Or do it. He looked into her eyes and saw a bone-deep weariness. And something else. Something that had nothing to do with comfort but everything to do with the heat between them. Because it was there, no matter how much he tried to ignore it.

"Maggie won't give you any trouble. I'll make sure of that."

"She means a lot to you, doesn't she?"

"I care about her, yeah. I told you, she's an old friend of mine." One of his oldest friends. Or she had been until she'd taken it into her head they needed to be more.

"I think she was more than that. You hooked up, didn't you?"

Hooked up. That wasn't what he'd have called it. "What does that have to do with anything?" he asked, a little annoyed.

"I knew it. There was something going on that

morning when I walked in on you two. She still has a thing for you."

He frowned at her. "No, she doesn't." He hoped. "What happened between us was over a long time ago."

"Right. You don't mean a thing to her. Which is why she hates me and wants to throw me in jail."

"She didn't throw you in jail. And she doesn't hate you." He said it to reassure himself as well as her.

"You are so clueless sometimes."

Maggie had called him dense. "If I promise to fix things with Maggie will you stay?"

She gazed at him a long moment. "I'll stay. I probably shouldn't. But I will."

"You're safe here, Delilah."

"I hope so."

"There's something else I wanted to talk to you about," he said. "I've got another job for you, in addition to waiting tables. If you want it."

"What is it?" she asked suspiciously.

God, didn't she trust him yet? "Payroll. It means a pay raise if you take over doing payroll for the restaurant." Cat had suggested it, because she knew how much Cam disliked doing it. And according to her, Delilah might not have an accounting degree, but she did have some experience. Enough to do his books. She'd be perfect to do it for him. Especially since, as his unsubtle youngest sister had put it, "You suck at it and I don't have time."

Delilah looked stunned. "You'd trust me to do payroll? To have access to your books?"

"I just said I would, didn't I?" Besides, he would be keeping an eye on them. But whatever secrets Delilah was keeping, and he knew there were some, he didn't believe she was a thief. "So, how about it?"

"I—I don't know what to say."

"Try yes. I have a small business payroll program on my computer." He got up. "Come on and I'll show you."

"What about lunch?"

"We've got time. Martha's here and so is George." George was one of the other bartenders. The two of them could handle business while he showed Delilah the program.

They went downstairs to his office where he pulled up the software. She came over to stand behind him. He ran through it and as he'd expected, she didn't have any problems with it.

"There's one thing we haven't talked about," she said after he finished.

"What's that?"

"Where are you going to put me? You're paying me in cash. What do you want me to do about that?"

He turned in his chair to look at her. "Since I've listed you as part-time help, you don't have to go anywhere."

She frowned. "But you're paying me for full-time work. Won't you get in trouble if you ever get audited?"

"Probably. But I don't expect to get audited."

"But you might." She bit her lip, worried it for a moment. "I don't want to get you in trouble because you helped me."

"Don't worry about it."

"I can't help it, I do worry."

God, she tempted him. She was close. All he had to do was lean forward an inch and he could taste her. Put his lips on her mouth, drink in the taste of her. He saw her mouth in his dreams, tasted her during the long, endless nights. Woke up hard and aching for her every morning.

She moistened her lips and whispered, "Cam?"

He pulled back abruptly. "We'd better get to work." He got the hell out of there before he blew every resolution he'd made into radioactive dust.

CAM WOULD HAVE LIKED to give Maggie another day to cool off, but he knew the sooner he talked to her, the better. He found her at the police station. It wasn't ideal, but he figured he could get her to take a coffee break. If she wasn't still ready to cut out his gizzard and fry it.

She looked up when he came in, but she didn't smile. She didn't look angry. She looked inscrutable. He was reminded that she'd always been a hell of a poker player.

"Hey, can you take a break?" he asked her.

Still unsmiling, she considered him for a moment. "All right." She got up and spoke to the other policeman. "I'm going for coffee."

Busy with paperwork, he waved her away. "Bring me some," he called after her. "And a doughnut too."

She waited until they were seated at a booth at the doughnut shop before she spoke. "What do you want, Cam?"

He opted for the direct approach. "Are you still mad at me?"

She frowned, then took a sip of coffee. Shrugged and said, "I guess not. You were right, it was a stupid idea."

"I wouldn't say it was stupid. Just not right for us."

"I feel like a fool."

"You shouldn't."

She lifted a shoulder. "I'll get over it."

"Do you want to tell me what that was all about?"

She sighed. "Lorna's pregnant again."

Her sister was younger than Maggie and already had two kids. This would be her third. "So what, you felt your biological clock ticking?"

She shot him a dirty look. "No. I heard her telling my parents that they'd better enjoy her kids because they'd probably never have any grandkids from me."

"Why does she think that? You're not exactly ancient."

"Hell, Cam, I haven't even had a date in months. It's not like there are men lined up dying to take me out." She snorted. "Much less marry me."

"You could date if you wanted," he said shrewdly. "You just don't want to."

"True. But I'm thinking about changing my mind on that. Let's not talk about it, okay?"

"Whatever you want."

"About the other day, can we just forget it ever happened?"

"Sure." He held out a hand. "Friends?"

"Friends," she echoed and shook it. She drank more coffee, watching him over the rim of the cup. "That's not all you wanted, is it?"

He'd thought long and hard about just how much of what he knew or suspected that he could tell Maggie. He didn't want to betray Delilah's confidences, but he didn't believe he could get Maggie to back off unless he told her something. "It's about Delilah."

"Surprise, surprise."

"I think she's in trouble."

"With the law?"

"No. She's running from an abusive boyfriend."

She studied him a moment. "And you think that because?"

"She told me. And I saw the bruises when she first got here." It still made him sick to think of those marks marring that beautiful skin.

"Does she want to press charges?"

He shook his head. "I tried to get her to do that, but she's terrified of the guy. She says she can't go to the police because then he'll find her."

"Which is why she wouldn't show me her license."

"Yeah. She's afraid he'd find out if you ran her through the system."

She drummed her fingers on the table. "How sure are you that she's telling you the truth? I know you said you saw the bruises but could they be explained another way?"

His gaze hardened. "The bastard tried to choke her. His fingerprints were on her neck."

"So, what are you asking me to do?"

"I'm asking you to do nothing. I don't want you to try to find out her background. At least until I can convince her to trust the police."

"It's not easy to find out much about her without a driver's license or social security number. I already ran her name and nothing popped."

"I'm asking you not to try to find out any more about her. For now."

"I don't like it," Maggie said, holding up a hand when he would have spoken. "If her story is true she should be in a shelter."

"Women aren't always safe there, are they?"

"Usually—" Maggie began.

"But not always. And she's scared to death. I know there's more to it but she won't tell me the whole story. Not yet. But she will."

Maggie's eyes widened. "My God, Cam, are you in love with this girl?"

"No." He denied it automatically, uneasily aware that lust wasn't the only thing he felt for Delilah. "I just want to help her."

Maggie looked unconvinced about that. "Be careful you don't get hurt while you're helping her."

"Will you do what I asked you?"

She hesitated, then nodded. "For you. But I still don't like it."

"Thanks, Maggie."

"The best thing you can do for her is get her to press charges and go to a shelter."

"I know. I'll try."

Now to tell Delilah that Maggie wouldn't be a problem. He had an idea that she wouldn't be happy with what he'd told Maggie, but he didn't see that he'd had any other choice.

CHAPTER NINE

"GOT A MINUTE?" Cam said.

Delilah jolted at the sound of his voice. She'd been folding napkins and daydreaming and hadn't realized he'd returned from his errand. "Sure." She followed him into his office.

"Have a seat."

Uneasiness prickled along her spine as she did as he'd suggested. "Why am I getting a bad feeling about this?"

"There's no need to. I just wanted to let you know you don't have to worry about Maggie. I talked to her and she agreed not to look into your background."

That was the last thing she'd expected to hear. "Just like that. Without even arguing."

He frowned. "Not exactly. I told her you were running from an abusive boyfriend."

For a minute she just stared at him. "You told her?" She jumped up out of the chair and paced the room. "How could you do that? I trusted you."

"I had to. I couldn't ask her not to check you out without giving her some kind of reason." He continued to frown at her.

"How do you know she'll do what you asked?"

"Because she said she would. I trust her, Delilah."

"Fine," she snapped. "I don't."

"Maggie agrees with me that the best thing for you to do would be to press charges."

"Maggie needs to mind her own business. And so do you." She left, knowing if she stayed she'd lose her temper. Besides, there was nothing to be done now but pray that Maggie Barnes kept her word to Cam.

A COUPLE OF DAYS LATER, Delilah went to Cam's office to work on the payroll. She shouldn't have stayed. If Maggie tried to find out more about her— But Maggie wasn't, by far, the only danger. She wasn't even the worst danger. Cam was. Or rather, her growing feelings for him were. How had he become so important to her, so quickly? Especially when she wasn't free to start a relationship.

She wasn't imagining his attraction to her. Or hers to him. He hadn't kissed her, hadn't done anything. Except look. Like he had that day when she'd forgotten her clothes and come out of the bathroom in a towel. His gaze had traveled over her in a slow sweep, top to bottom, and then had stayed on her chest. When he'd met her eyes, she'd seen desire darkening them to a deep gray. And she'd felt an answering response, deep inside. After that brief moment, though, he'd mumbled a curse and disappeared into the bathroom.

But the look in his eyes had said what he wouldn't.

The door opened, startling her. Gabe Randolph came in. He looked as surprised to see her as she was to see him. "Cam's not here," she said quickly. She didn't feel very comfortable with Gabe. He'd made it pretty clear he didn't like her and thought she was up to no good.

"I can see that." His eyes narrowed. "The question is, what are you doing here when he's not?"

Ignoring his belligerent tone, she said sweetly, "I don't really see that's any of your business."

His face darkened and he stepped forward. "What the hell are you doing with the restaurant checkbook?"

"I'm working on payroll. Satisfied?"

"Not by a long shot. Cam gave you access to the Scarlet Parrot's books?"

"Obviously. Unlike you, he doesn't think I'm going to rob him blind."

"Unlike me, Cam's a damn sight too trusting."

She got up and glared at him. "This is Cam's business, not yours. You need to take it up with him."

"Don't worry, sweetheart, that's exactly what I'm going to do." He turned away and strode to the door, then paused to look back at her.

"You think you've got it pretty cushy here, don't you? I wouldn't count on that continuing forever."

He slammed the door shut. She picked up a box of papers and threw it at the door. Then she cursed herself for letting him get to her and went to clean up the mess.

UNTIL DELILAH STARTED WORKING for him, Cam hadn't realized how wearing it was never to be able to leave the restaurant without worrying. Martha was a hard worker, and honest, but she was more of a worker bee than a manager. He never felt comfortable leaving her totally alone with the restaurant for long periods. With Delilah being there, it was a different matter. She could handle whatever came up, at least until Cam returned.

Delilah was fast becoming indispensable. He wondered what he would do when she left. Because she would leave. If she'd had her way, she'd already be gone. Once she got on her feet again, he wouldn't be able to keep her there.

He should be glad of that. But he wasn't.

It was early afternoon when he came in after running some of the errands that in the past he'd had to put off until Mondays. Gabe was sitting at the bar, drinking a beer and scowling.

"Hey, what's going on?" Cam asked, coming around behind the bar.

"Where the hell have you been and are you crazy?"

Cam gave him a closer look, wondering what Gabe was so bent out of shape about. "I've been out and last time I checked, no, I'm not crazy." He looked around and saw Martha, waiting on the lone table of customers, but not Delilah. "Have you seen Delilah?"

Gabe scowled, his face darkening. "Yeah, I've seen her. She's in your office. Messing with your books. Doing your payroll, for God's sake."

Cam picked up his mug and filled it. "And that's a problem for you, why?"

"Your problem, not mine," Gabe snapped. "You're asking for trouble. You're giving her carte blanche to embezzle from you. Dumb-ass."

Cam laughed as he set the beer in front of Gabe. "First of all, I see the books, too. And so will Cat come tax time. They're pretty straightforward. It would be easy to tell if someone was skimming. Besides, I trust Delilah."

"Why?" Gabe shot at him. "You took her in off the street. You don't know anything about her."

"I know enough." He knew she still had secrets, but her basic honesty wasn't a concern. "You're just pissed because she turned you down."

Gabe rolled his eyes. "Like I've never been turned down before? That's not my objection to her. I know the type. She's out to get something, Cam. Watch out she doesn't take you for a ride."

He knew Gabe was only worried because he cared about him, but Gabe's attitude still irritated him. "It's not like I'm rich. What do you think she's after?"

"I don't know. But trust me, you don't have to be rich to have a woman con you."

"Delilah's not trying to con me. I know a con when I see one."

"Normally, I'd agree with you." He took a long drink of his beer and slapped the glass down. "But not this time." He pointed his finger at him and jabbed it for emphasis. "You're hot for her, that's your problem. And your judgment's all shot because of that."

"What is it with my family? I'm not hot for Delilah." Like hell he wasn't, but he wouldn't admit it to Gabe or anyone else. "I can help a woman without having the hots for her." He started putting up glassware, hanging it in the overhead racks while he tried to think of a way to get rid of his brother.

"Sure you can." Gabe studied him for a moment, then leaned forward. "So tell me, Cam, how long has it been since you had a date?"

"I don't know." But he did. He knew exactly. "What does that have to do with anything?"

"You haven't had a date since Delilah moved in with you. Have you?"

He shrugged. "Coincidence. I've been busy."

"You've never been too busy for women before. You're too busy to go out because you're obsessed with getting into Delilah's pants."

Cam's temper snapped, spurred on by the fact that his brother was absolutely right. He grabbed hold of Gabe's shirt. Only the fact that they were in his restaurant and there were customers around kept Cam from slugging him. "Shut up, Gabe."

"Oh, I'm done. I'd say I just proved my point."

Forget the customers. He might just punch him anyway. "You haven't proved a damn thing other than that you're an incredible ass."

"Don't let me interrupt, but you might want to take that outside," Delilah said from behind Cam.

Both Cam and Gabe looked at her. "That's what you always tell the customers," she said, keeping her eyes on Cam.

He couldn't tell if she'd heard what Gabe had said or not. He was tempted to do what she said and just have it out with his brother. Anything to release some of the frustration he'd been living with since Delilah had come to stay. But he was too old to pound the hell out of Gabe, no matter how much his brother might deserve it.

"We're finished," he said, and let go of Gabe's shirt. "Get lost, Gabe."

Gabe looked like he was about to say something, but after giving Delilah a dirty look and Cam a disgusted one, he threw some money down on the bar. "See you around, sucker," he said, and left.

They were both silent, then Delilah sighed. "He really doesn't like me, does he?"

"Why do you think that was about you?"

"Call it a hunch. I'm right, aren't I?"

Cam didn't answer directly. He picked up the dirty mug and dumped the leftover beer, then dropped it in the soapy water. "Ignore him. Sometimes Gabe is a jerk."

"He's sort of hard to ignore. A little while ago he came into the office and freaked out when he saw I was doing your books."

"He'll get over it." To give himself something to do, he polished the bar.

"He thinks I'm going to steal from you. He practically accused me of theft. I thought he was going to call the cops right then and there." She laughed without humor. "Maggie Barnes would have loved that."

She was trying to act indifferent, but he heard the note of anxiety in her voice. "Delilah." He caught her hand and squeezed it gently. "I know you wouldn't do anything like that, and that's what matters. I told you, ignore him."

She gazed at him, her expression troubled. Then she looked down at their joined hands before raising her eyes to his. "Was it true?"

"Was what true?"

"What Gabe said. Do you want to get into my pants?"

CHAPTER TEN

HE DROPPED HER HAND as if it had scalded him. She might have laughed, but she didn't find it remotely amusing.

He looked angry, not uncomfortable. "So you heard that, did you?"

"Yes." And hated herself that her first reaction, her gut reaction, had been to hope it was true.

He turned away, pulling a towel out of his back pocket and wiping the spotless bar. "I've told you before, all I expect from you is for you to do your job."

Don't push it, she told herself. *This thing between you can't go anywhere. You know it can't.* But she couldn't let it go. "That's all you expect," she agreed. She waited a moment, then added, "But what do you want?"

She'd asked him that before, and he'd denied wanting anything more than a platonic relationship with her. But judging from his brother's reaction, he was worried Cam wanted more.

For a long moment Cam stared at her blankly, then muttered a curse and left her.

She blew out a shaky breath. Oh, Lord, she was in trouble. Deep trouble.

"What was that all about?" Martha asked her as she came to get her drink orders. "I'm not sure I've ever seen Cam and Gabe go at it like that."

Back in control, Delilah shook her head. "Some brother thing, I guess."

"Or a woman thing," Martha said shrewdly. "I've got eyes, haven't I?" she added when Delilah looked at her quizzically. "You like him, don't you? Cam, I mean."

Unfortunately, yes. But she answered nonchalantly. "Everybody likes Cam. What's not to like?"

"You know what I mean. And so does Gabe. He's been on your case since you got here."

"I'm not interested in Cam and he's not interested in me," she said flatly, knowing it was a lie. "Whatever his brother thinks."

"If you say so, sweetie."

"What's with Gabe, anyway? Why doesn't he like me? At first I thought it was because I turned him down when he asked me out, but I don't really think that's it."

"Oh, probably something to do with Cam's broken heart." Martha set her tray down and started fill-ing a drink order. "Gabe doesn't want him hurt again. He must be afraid of what you'll do."

"Cam has a broken heart?" News to her. He didn't act like a man with a broken heart.

Martha nodded. "Used to, anyway. On account of his fiancée."

Fiancée? She'd known he'd never been married. He'd said nothing about having been engaged.

"Let me take these drinks and drop off my order and we'll talk," Martha promised as she hefted the tray.

But they never did. Business picked up and both of them got busy. Cameron got busy, too, she noticed as the evening wore on. He put a lot of effort into flirting with every pretty female who came in. They didn't seem to mind. Delilah had seen him flirt before, and she knew from several sources that he dated a lot of women. Not that he had since she'd come to live with him. Still, this time seemed different. All that flirting seemed a little forced.

Right. *Wishful thinking, Delilah.*

She had no right to the jealousy his flirting caused her. No right at all. What Cam did was his business, and none of hers. Let him romance all the women he wanted. She should be glad. Glad he wasn't coming on to her.

But she wasn't.

If only she'd never met Avery. If she could have met Cam, gotten to know him without the secrets between them. Cam couldn't be more different than Avery. Cam was about as true blue as they came. *Don't forget hot,* she reminded herself, watching him serve another woman a drink.

Avery was good-looking. On the outside. Inside he was pure evil. She shook off the memories, praying she'd never have cause to think about him again. She had escaped. Once again she felt guilty because she hadn't done anything about her suspicions. But they were just that, suspicions. And unlike Avery's poor first wife, she was alive and meant to stay that way.

THE FOLLOWING MONDAY, Delilah walked into the kitchen to find Cam on the phone.

"Tell him I'll take him soon," he said. "When he's not throwing up. Talk to you later. Good luck." He hung up and said, "Poor bastard."

"Who?"

"Mark. I was going to take Max to the Texas State Aquarium in Corpus Christi, but he's got a virus. They've *all* got the virus." A corner of his mouth lifted. "Except Mark. Poor bastard has to take care of them all."

"You could offer to help him," Delilah said mischievously.

He looked at her in mock horror. "Are you kidding? They're all throwing up. I don't feel *that* sorry for him."

They both laughed at that.

"What's the aquarium like?" Delilah asked. "I guess it must be big if it's the Texas State Aquarium. I went to the Houston Aquarium years ago, but I don't remember much."

"It's pretty cool. Why don't you go with me?"

Delilah was startled at just how badly she wanted to accept the casual invitation. But she knew she shouldn't. "I wasn't asking for an invitation. I'm sure you have other things you'd rather be doing."

"I like the aquarium. Why do you think I offered to take Max?"

"Because you're a really nice man."

His mouth lifted in amusement. "Boy, have I got you fooled. Nope. I go because I enjoy it. I take all my nieces and nephews."

"I…shouldn't."

"Why not? We've got the day off and nothing urgent to do. Come on, it'll be fun."

Fun. It would be fun, but mostly because she'd be going with Cam. *Don't do it, Delilah. It's practically a date and you have no business going.* No business having fun. No business enjoying herself. No business enjoying Cam's company as much as she did.

"Give me ten minutes to get ready," she said, and hoped she wasn't making a huge mistake.

"What do you want to see first?" he asked her when they arrived.

"I have no idea. Surprise me."

And he did. He not only knew the exhibits, he knew a good many of the people who worked there. They started in the Back Bay Marsh, with the alligators and moved on through the exhibit where they rehabbed birds, sea turtles and marine mammals. They stopped at the hermit crab exhibit and saw some children picking them up under the guidance of the staff.

"Go on," Cam said. "You know you want to."

She let him talk her into it and was promptly fascinated by the creature. The sea-horse exhibit came next and Cam told her about them, mentioning that the male sea horse carried the eggs.

"How do you know all this?" He'd told her something about every exhibit. She'd had no idea he knew so much about marine life.

"When you've been as many times as I have, you have it memorized."

"Did you really bring Max here?" she asked, thinking of the busy little boy and the acres of glass. It took a brave man to do that. "I can't imagine."

"The first time was an experience." Cam laughed.

"He was barely three. He went through the place in thirty-seven seconds flat, with me chasing behind him."

"But it's huge."

"Okay, that's a slight exaggeration, but he's a speedy little devil. He's gotten better now that he's a bit older. Thank God."

Delilah thought it was a shame that a man who so obviously loved children didn't have any of his own. It didn't seem to bother him, though. He'd told her early on that he had no interest in marriage or kids of his own.

They spent the day there, wandering through exhibits that held sharks and groupers, sea turtles, and a coral reef with a rainbow of colors. Cam laughed when she turned around and, finding herself face to face with a moray eel, shrieked and grabbed his arm.

"You're as much fun to bring as the kids." He gave her hair a tug and smiled. Slowly, his smile faded as their gazes held. His hand slipped beneath her hair to the nape of her neck. His eyes darkened and that look came into them, the one she'd seen before. The one that said he wanted her.

For an instant she forgot everything. All the reasons she shouldn't have come, all the reasons she couldn't have him, all the reasons she shouldn't be standing there willing him to kiss her. For an endless moment she was simply a woman having a wonderful day with a man she could be falling in love with.

And she was bound to a man who would kill her if he found her.

Cam's hand dropped, she turned away. And pain blossomed in her heart.

The moment had passed, but Delilah didn't believe either of them would forget it.

They ended the afternoon with the dolphin tank. "I think the dolphins are my favorite," she told Cam. "But I liked all of it." She smiled at him, wishing she could tell him what the day had meant to her. "Thank you for bringing me."

"Day's not over yet. What are you in the mood to eat?" Cam asked.

"I don't care as long as there's plenty of it. I'm starving." She shouldn't be since she'd eaten junk all afternoon, but she was.

He took her to a place she could only describe as a dive. The parking lot was poorly lit, the building little more than a dilapidated shack with a sign she could barely make out. "Hushpuppy's?"

"Yeah, don't let the outside fool you. This is some of the best fried shrimp and hush puppies on the coast. They just don't believe in wasting money on the surroundings."

"I can see that. But if you say it's good, it's okay with me." She arched a brow and asked him, "Is the food better than your place?"

"The shrimp and hush puppies are, but I'll call you a liar if you tell anyone I said that."

She laughed and crossed her heart. "I won't, I promise."

"We can go someplace nicer if you want," he said. "Not too nice, since we're not dressed for it."

She looked down at her jeans. "This is fine. I'm sure I'll like it. Besides, I don't even own a dress. Not anymore. Not since——" She closed her eyes and shook her head to clear the image.

"Don't do that."

"Do what?"

"Think about him."

"How did you know?"

He raised his hand to her cheek, stroked his fingers gently down it until they reached her mouth. His thumb slid over her lips in a whisper touch. "Because you look so sad," he finally said. "No one as young and pretty as you should have a sorrow that big."

She didn't know what to say, so she said nothing. Her stomach jittered and she wished... His hand dropped, they got out of the truck and went inside.

She wouldn't have thought it from the outside, but the place was romantic. Far too romantic for someone with no intention of having a romance with the man beside her. They found a seat in a dark corner, with a flickering candle on the table giving off a meager light.

"Why do you want to be a CPA?" Cam asked her, referring to the conversation they'd begun on the way to the restaurant.

The waitress slapped a bowl of hush puppies and a couple of draft beers down on the table and hustled off.

"I like numbers. No, I love numbers. They're—" She thought about it a moment. "They're fun."

"So Cat says. She likes it, but I think she likes re-habbing birds better."

Delilah bit into a hush puppy, remembering how much Cat had seemed to enjoy it when they'd talked about accounting. According to her, her family changed the subject whenever she brought it up, so she'd quit trying.

"Rehabbing birds is a cool career. You can see she loves it. I wouldn't want to do something I hated for the rest of my life. Would you?"

"No, which is why I own a restaurant instead of being an accountant."

"You really love the restaurant business, don't you?"

"Yeah. I can't see doing anything else. I like the people. That's one reason I tend bar. You see an interesting slice of life as a bartender."

They stayed talking long after their meal was finished. Finally, Cam signaled for the check and they left.

She didn't want the day to end. She didn't want to go to the apartment where he would go to his bed and she to hers. She didn't want to lie alone in her bed and damn fate for having sent Avery to her first.

"You want to have a nightcap?" he asked her when they got to the Scarlet Parrot.

"The bar's closed."

"I have an in with the owner."

"Cute." But she smiled and went up the stairs to the restaurant. It was a mistake, she didn't doubt, as she watched him pour brandy into two glasses. But she'd been making them all day and didn't think one more would do much harm. Even if she had nothing else, she'd have memories of a beautiful day.

He put the glasses on the bar and came around to sit beside her. He'd left the place in shadows, with a single light burning. The night was quiet, with the faint whisper of a fan the only sound breaking it.

Cam swirled the liquor in the glass, then took a sip. "The night you broke in was my fortieth birthday. I was alone because I was bored out of my mind with the women I'd been dating."

"Why do you date them, then?"

He shot her a sideways glance and a corner of his mouth lifted in amusement. "They're not always boring."

She laughed and he went on. "At first I thought you were a kid. Maybe a runaway." His gaze traveled slowly over her. "But you're not a kid."

She shook her head. "No."

"It would be better for both of us if you were."

"Yes," she said huskily. "But I'm not."

His palm cupped her cheek. His thumb traced her mouth, as it had earlier that night when he'd talked about the sorrow he saw in her eyes. "If you keep looking at me like that I'm going to kiss you," he murmured. "Are you sure you want to start down that road?"

Oh, she wanted to. Desperately. But she couldn't. She was no naive child, she knew exactly where a kiss would lead them. To his bed. To making love with him. And she knew in her heart it would be wonderful.

And it would be a lie.

She got up and went upstairs without another word.

CHAPTER ELEVEN

THE RAIN CAME IN at closing time. Cam sent Martha home before it grew worse, though he knew an urge to keep her around. He didn't want to be alone with Delilah.

Like hell he didn't. He wanted to be alone with her, but he knew he shouldn't. Look what had nearly happened the last time they'd been alone. Why had he thought he could spend the day with her and not want to make love to her? If she hadn't left when she had, she'd have been in his bed.

He had to remind himself why that was such a bad idea.

He should help her look for another place to stay, but that wasn't going to happen on her salary and given the sparsity of places to rent in Aransas City. But damn, he hadn't realized how hard it would be to live with a woman he couldn't have. Why would he? He hadn't lived with a woman since he'd left his childhood home.

He thought about Delilah wearing the towel. He couldn't stop thinking about it. She'd been so beautiful. Tempting. A flick of his wrist and she'd have been naked. And he'd have been lost. He knew she hadn't done it on purpose, but his poor, starved libido didn't care.

Worse than that, though, had been the day at the aquarium. Because that hadn't been about sex. Sex was normal; he could deal with wanting her. But damn, he liked her. He'd had a blast showing her one of his favorite places, a place he'd never taken a woman. A place he'd always reserved for his family. Until Delilah.

Worse yet, he'd enjoyed talking to her, enjoyed being with her. He was damned near obsessed with her and he'd never even kissed her.

Shit, he was in trouble.

"I'm going to deposit the cash," he said, glad for an excuse to leave.

"I'll go with you," Delilah said. Before he could answer, she went out and came back with the sweatshirt she'd been wearing the first night he saw her.

He picked up the bank bag and frowned at her. "I don't need any help. The bank is only a few blocks away."

"That's okay. I just need a change of scene." She

smiled at him. "Come on, Cam, take me with you. Please?"

He gave up. A short while later, with the interior of the truck warming up, the rain tapping a soft song on the windshield, and her sexy scent wrapping around him like a woman's arms, he wished he hadn't. He gritted his teeth, deciding silence was his best course.

Delilah turned on the stereo. Chris Isaak was singing about a solitary man, a soft, sad lament. They listened for a bit and Delilah said, "That song reminds me of you."

Puzzled, he glanced at her. "Why? I'm not solitary."

"Yes, you are. You have a core of solitude. It's always there, even when you're with other people."

"Thank you, Dr. Phil."

"Scoff all you want, but I think it's true. You don't want anyone to reach you. You don't even carry a cell phone."

"That has nothing to do with solitude. I don't have a cell phone because if I did, Martha or my family would be calling me every ten seconds. When I leave the restaurant I want to get away. Having a cell phone defeats the purpose."

"Convenient excuse to do just what you want. Cut yourself off." When he didn't reply she continued, "You're that way with women, too. There's a part of you that says, back off, don't touch."

He shot her an irritated glance before looking back at the road. "How would you know that?"

"Aside from the fact that you told me yourself the women you date bore you silly?"

He'd forgotten he'd told her that. "Yeah, aside from that."

"Your reputation precedes you. I hear you give a woman two months, tops. That's not long enough for anyone to get to know you."

He laughed. "I wouldn't say that."

"I'm not talking about sex. I'm talking about intimacy."

"I'd say sex was about as intimate as you can get."

She was quiet a moment, then said in a tight voice. "Not always."

Damn, he didn't want to go there. Uncomfortable with the turn of conversation, he shifted. "Is there a reason you're dissecting my personal life?" He reached the bank and drove to the night deposit window.

"I—you're right. I shouldn't be. I'm sorry."

Now he felt like a jerk. "No, you're right. I don't like women to get too close."

"Because of your ex-fiancée?"

In the middle of getting his receipt, he turned to stare at her. "Who told you about her?"

"Martha. She didn't tell me much. Just that your fiancée broke your heart."

He snorted and rolled up his window. "She didn't break my heart." Janine had told him he didn't have one to break. As if that justified what she'd done.

"What happened?" She sounded sympathetic, not simply curious.

He pulled away from the window and headed home. He opted for the short version. "I found her in bed with a friend of mine. End of engagement."

"And the friendship?"

His smile wasn't nice. "End of that, too."

She was silent for a long moment. "She betrayed you and you couldn't forgive that."

"It's not a matter of forgiving. I don't think it says much for your chances of a successful marriage if your prospective wife cheats on you before you ever get married."

"What if you'd been married? Would you have forgiven her then?"

"It's a moot point. I didn't marry her. Which I'm damned glad of. She lied, she cheated and that was enough for me."

"So you've crossed women off."

At the stop sign he turned to stare at her incredulously. "Listen, sugar, I don't know who you've been talking to, but if you think I've been celibate for the last twelve years, think again."

"I didn't say you'd crossed sex off your list. I said you'd crossed off women. Serious relationships, anyway. However many women you've slept with, you haven't gotten married or even engaged again, have you?"

He ground his teeth, unwilling to admit she had a point. Besides, all this talk of sex was getting to him. "And you know all about what motivates me from your vast life experience?" he asked.

"I may not have *vast* experience, but I have a lot more than you think." She snapped the words and he could tell he'd annoyed her.

"My mother and I didn't have much, and what we did have we worked for. I've been working since I was ten years old and got my first paper route. And I've been on my own since I was sixteen. You grow up fast when you're in foster care, and then out in the real world."

"Maybe. But you're still young."

She sighed. "Old enough to have made some huge mistakes."

They pulled into the carport under the restaurant. The song turned to a commercial and Delilah changed the channel. An old Garth Brooks tune was playing. "Every Time That It Rains." Great. Garth began singing about dresses falling off and making love in the rain. Cam started sweating, wishing he didn't have such a vivid imagination. Wishing he could remember the last time he'd been with a woman. All he knew was it had been too damn long.

"Everyone makes mistakes. God knows, I've made them. But I haven't been nursing a broken heart for twelve years. And I don't think all women are manipulative liars and cheats." Most of them, yes.

"Don't you?" He heard the click as her seat belt released. "For a long time I thought everyone was like…him. Or at least, I thought all men were like him."

"But you don't now."

"No."

She touched his arm. Just a touch but he felt it like an electric shock.

"Something changed my mind. Someone." He looked at her and their gazes locked. "You changed my mind, Cam."

Her voice was husky. It reminded him of the first night he'd seen her. Worse, it made him think of damp sheets and sweaty sex. He looked away. He hadn't thought about another woman for more than five minutes since Delilah had come into his life.

Would it be so bad to take what was happening between them to its natural conclusion?

You bet your ass it would.

Delilah wasn't like the women who'd occupied his bed in the last twelve years. Those women had been forgettable. Enjoyable, but ultimately, forgettable. Delilah was anything but. She'd already gotten to him, and it was just getting worse the longer he knew her.

Maybe if he ignored it, they could forget this little moment had ever happened. Hell, they could forget the entire conversation had happened. He still couldn't believe he'd been talking about his sex life to a woman he'd sworn not to take to bed.

He wanted to make love to her until neither of them could think. And though he hadn't lost his mind yet, she was pushing him dangerously close to it. He put his hands on her arms and pulled her closer. Her mouth was close. Moist and so inviting he wanted to plunge in, kiss her until neither of them could breathe. Make love to her, not just once, but all night. And he wanted to do it all over again the next night. And the next.

"This is a mistake." His mind knew that, but his body didn't give a damn.

"I know."

"Once I kiss you, there's no going back."

"I know that, too." She swallowed, blew out a breath. "Let me go, Cam. Before...before it's too late."

"Maybe it already is," he said, but he let her go. He turned off the truck and got out, waiting for her to catch up with him. Neither spoke.

He opened the door and let her in, then locked up behind her and headed upstairs. There was a light burning in the restaurant kitchen and he started to turn it off.

"Cam—"

Whatever she'd been going to say, the ring of the telephone cut her off. He was tempted to ignore it but then his mother's voice came over the answering machine.

"Cameron, are you there?" Her voice sounded odd. Quivery, which wasn't like her at all. Cam went to the wall phone and picked up the receiver. "I'm here. What's wrong, Mom?"

"Oh, thank God you're there," his mother said on a sob. "I think I'm having a heart attack."

CHAPTER TWELVE

DELILAH SAW THE BLOOD DRAIN from Cam's face as he talked to his mother. Bad news, obviously. His next words confirmed it.

"Did you call 9-1-1?" He waited a moment, then said, "Typical. Okay, forget EMT. Did you take an aspirin? Mom, stop crying and listen to me. Take an aspirin, then call one of the neighbors on your cell phone and ask them to take you to the hospital. If they can't, I'll come get you. Just do it, right now. I'll stay on the line."

While he waited, he said to Delilah, "My mother thinks she's having a heart attack."

"Oh, Cam, I'm sorry."

"Damn EMT said it would be an hour before they get there."

"Why don't you go get her?"

"I would, but she lives twenty minutes away, in the opposite direction from the hospital. It will be quicker if she can get—" He broke off and spoke into the phone. "Yeah, I'm here. Good, I'll see you there. And I'll call everyone." He smiled for the first time since he'd answered the phone. "You know they'd kill me if I didn't call them. Don't worry, I'm sure you'll be fine. I love you, too, Mom."

He hung up and for a long moment he stood there, staring blindly.

"Cam?" She went to him and patted his arm. "Are you all right? Can I do something?"

He looked at her but didn't seem to see her. "My father—" He didn't say any more.

Delilah had never seen him so shaken before. He was always strong and in control, but he sure wasn't now. "What about your father?"

"He died of a heart attack." He looked so bleak and so lost, she just wanted to hug him. He scrubbed his hands over his face and with a visible effort, pulled himself together. "I have to call my brother and sisters."

She waited while he called all of them. She didn't want to intrude, but she wanted to help him, any way she could.

"I don't know when I'll be back," he said after he hung up from talking to his sister Cat.

"I'm going with you." He looked surprised. "In fact, I think you should let me drive. You're obviously upset."

"You can't drive my truck. It's a stick shift."

"I've already driven it, remember?"

"I forgot." He picked up his keys. "It doesn't matter. I can drive, Delilah. I'm upset, not incompetent."

Maybe he needed to drive, needed to feel in control. "All right. Do you want me to come with you?"

He hesitated. "You don't have to do that."

"I don't mind." She was prepared to argue with him about that, all night if necessary. No matter what he said, she didn't think he should be alone. She knew from personal experience how it felt to be all alone when one of your loved ones was desperately ill. Once he got to the hospital and his brother and sisters were there, he'd be all right, but until then she was sticking to him like white on rice.

"Thanks."

They got in the truck and pulled out. Delilah was glad to see it had stopped raining. After the first couple of miles of silence, Cam said, "My mother's always been so healthy. I can't believe she has heart problems and we didn't even know it. She's never had any symptoms before."

"Maybe she doesn't. Maybe it's a false alarm."

"I guess it could be." He didn't sound too sure of that. "My dad didn't know, but then, he never went to the doctor if he could help it. He was alone, out on his boat when it happened. When he never showed up, my mother sent the coast guard after him. He was gone by the time they got there. He never had a chance."

"But your mother is getting help. Wasn't it a good sign that she was talking to you? It couldn't be too severe, could it?" She didn't know, but there was no point in him torturing himself all the way to the hospital when there wasn't a thing he could do.

"I don't know. I don't know much about it. She said her chest hurt and she was afraid it was a heart attack." His hands tightened on the steering wheel. "This is the first time I've wished I had a cell phone. I could ask Jay some of these questions if I did."

She had met Jay, his brother-in-law who was a doctor, when he came into the restaurant with Gail and their kids. "Will he be at the hospital?"

"Yes, I told Gail to ask him to come. They'll probably leave all the kids with Mark so Cat and Gail can both come to the hospital."

"Your family is very close. That must be nice." She couldn't imagine what that was like, having a family to depend on.

"Not always," he said, laughing a little. "They tend to butt into my business more than I'd like."

Like Gabe, she thought, but she didn't think she needed to bring that up. "I used to wish I had a brother or sister. I pestered my mother about it for a long time, but she said I was enough for her. I don't know how I expected it to happen, anyway. She didn't date much, much less have a serious relationship."

"What happened to your dad?"

She laughed humorlessly. "Oh, he was a winner. He abandoned my mother when she found out she was pregnant. She was sixteen. Her parents threw her out of the house. It's a miracle she managed to have me and support us. She never talked much about that time, but I know it was rough."

He glanced at her. "Sorry, I didn't mean to bring up sad subjects."

"It's not, really. It all happened before I was born. And I had my mom, and she was enough."

"What did she—" He broke off and swore. "Never mind."

"Cancer. That's what you were going to ask, isn't it?" Such a simple word for such a world of hurt. And it still hurt, would always hurt, she knew. Just as she would always miss her. But she had learned to deal with her mother's death. She'd had no other choice but to accept it, and go on.

"Yeah. I'm sorry."

"It's okay." She knew he was grasping at anything to take his mind off his own mother. And she also knew that nothing would relieve his mind until he found out his mother was all right.

"Thanks for coming with me." He reached for her hand and held it resting on his thigh.

"You're welcome," she said and her throat felt tight. "She'll be all right, Cam."

"I hope so."

He held her hand the rest of the way to the hospital.

THEY WERE THE FIRST ONES to arrive at the hospital. His mother arrived a short time after them, before Cam had managed to wear a hole in the floor pacing.

Meredith Randolph was a pretty blond woman who looked at least ten years younger than Delilah knew she had to be. She burst into tears when she saw her son. It was clear from her demeanor that she depended a great deal on her oldest son. It was equally clear that Cam was crazy about her.

Delilah watched as the familiar Cam slid back into place, the one who took care of everyone else, the one they all depended on. She didn't think anyone realized, least of all Cam, that no one returned the favor. Unless you counted Gabe trying to protect Cam from her. But that was another story.

The fact was, Cam didn't think he needed help, and he'd have been the first to reject it.

A few minutes later a nurse wheeled Mrs. Randolph away and Cam left his mother long enough to talk to Delilah. "They're putting her in an exam room and I'm going with her. Her doctor is on the way, but tell Jay to come back and find us when he gets here, okay?"

"All right." She wanted to say something comforting but nothing came to mind. The only things she thought of were stupid, useless things, like try not to worry. As she watched him walk away, she tried her best not to think about another hospital. Another mother.

She didn't have long to wait before the others got there. Jay, Gail and Cat all came in at once. Jay left them to go to the desk, and Gail and Cat spotted her and came over to where she had been sitting in an uncomfortable hard plastic waiting-room chair.

"Delilah, are you here with Cam?" Gail asked. Delilah started to answer but Gail rushed on. "Never mind, of course you are."

"Where are they?" Cat asked. "Do you know what happened? What's going on?"

Delilah shook her head. "I don't know any more than you do. They took your mother back a few minutes ago, right after she got here. Cam went with her. He asked if Jay would come back there." She pointed to the double doors that led to the examining rooms.

Gail turned as her husband approached. "Delilah says Cam and Mom are in the exam room."

"I know," Jay said. "Why don't you two wait here and I'll see what I can find out. Then—"

"Forget it, Jay," Cat interrupted heatedly. "We're going to see our mother. Now."

Gail rubbed his arm and looked at him, but didn't say anything.

He shrugged, apparently not much surprised. "All right. Let's go."

Delilah barely had time to sit down again before Gabe came striding through the emergency room entrance. She cursed under her breath, wishing one of his sisters was there to deal with him. She was the last person he'd want to see right now.

He hadn't noticed her yet and she had time to observe him without the distraction of listening to him or feeling that glacial demeanor that came over him when he looked at her. He was a good-looking guy, she had to admit. Dark, like his sister Cat, but tall, like his brother. What her mother had always called go-to-hell looks. He was probably even nice. To some people. People whose guts he didn't hate.

He spotted her and his expression changed from

worried to angry. He was at her side in a few hasty strides. He towered over her, disapproval radiating from him.

"I should have known you'd be here. Where's Cam? And where's my mother?"

She simply pointed to the double doors.

"Why are you here? Never mind," he said when she started to answer. "I don't want to hear it." He turned his back and strode toward the doors.

"I came here with Cam because I was worried about him." Although why she bothered trying to tell Gabe anything, she didn't know. He'd made up his mind about her the first time they met and she didn't believe anything short of a baseball bat to the head would change it.

He turned around, giving her a cynical look. "Worried? Right. Save it for somebody more gullible."

Just then Gail and Cat came back through the doors and Gabe went to meet them. Delilah watched them together, feeling more uncomfortable and out of place by the minute. Cam was with his mother, he didn't need her here. The rest of the Randolphs sure as heck didn't need her either.

She was debating whether to leave when Cat motioned for her to come over. Unlike Gabe, Cam's sisters seemed to like her.

"How's your mother doing? Have they found anything out yet?" she asked Cat, who kept glancing worriedly at the double doors.

"No, but she's feeling a little better." She frowned and looked at Gail. "I wish she'd let us stay with her, but she threw us all out. Except Cam."

"You know Cam will calm her down better than anyone," Gail said. "Besides, she doesn't want us, she wants him."

"I know. She always says she doesn't have a favorite of her children, but she does. Especially—" Cat's voice cracked and she tried again. "When something bad happens."

Gail twisted her hands together nervously. "Jay says the emergency room doctor who's treating her is very good."

Gabe stuck his hands in his pockets and stared at the door. "Seems like she should have a heart specialist if it's her heart," he said.

"They don't know what's wrong yet," Cat said. "It might be nothing. We'll get her a specialist if we need to." She patted Gabe's arm. "Don't think about it, Gabe."

"I'm not thinking about anything," Gabe snapped, jerking away from her.

"Of course you are," Cat said. "We're all thinking about Dad. How can we help thinking about him?"

"I'd been doing fine until you brought it up. Can't you ever just not talk?"

Cat looked as upset and angry as her brother. She opened her mouth to answer him, but Gail stopped her with a gesture. "Gabe." Gail put herself between the two and tried to make peace. "We're all upset, yelling at each other isn't going to help."

Gabe just shrugged and didn't say anything while Cat and Gail went to sit down. Delilah hesitated, unsure what to do, but wanting to make Gabe feel better. She didn't think he meant to be a jerk to his sister. It was clear he was upset about their mother.

"It's hard waiting," she said to him. "I know how hard it is."

He glanced at her. "Thanks, but keep your sympathy. Do me a favor and leave me alone," he added. "While you're at it, leave Cam alone, too."

Hurt, she sucked in a breath. "Tell me something, Gabe. Why do you hate me?"

He rolled his eyes. "Spare me the drama queen act. I don't hate you. I wouldn't care what you did if you weren't playing my brother."

"I'm not playing him. Do you really think I'd take advantage of him after what he's done for me?"

He smiled. It wasn't a nice smile. "Oh, yeah, baby. In a heartbeat."

"Why do you think he needs you to look out for him? He seems pretty self-sufficient to me. Don't you think he's smart enough to take care of himself?"

"Usually. But women have a way of messing with the best of us."

"And that would be you?"

"No, that would be my brother."

"I'm not looking to hurt him."

"Right. That's what they all say. And then they walk away and leave you bleeding."

"Is that what happened to you?" she asked him, light suddenly dawning. Gabe was worried about Cam all right, but she didn't believe it was because of Cam's failed engagement. No, it was more personal than that. She wondered just what had made Gabe so cynical. And so distrustful of women.

"We're talking about Cam, not me."

"Are we?"

"Gabe, what's the matter with you? Why are you being so rude to Delilah?" Gail had come over in time to catch at least some of the conversation. She turned to Delilah. "Ignore him, he gets like this when he's upset. I'm glad Cam had someone to drive over here with."

Gabe muttered something and stalked away. Thankfully, Delilah hadn't understood it, but she could guess the meaning and it wasn't particularly conciliatory.

She blew out a breath. "Well, this is awkward."

"I know. I'm sorry. Come sit with me," Gail said. "Cat's gone to call Mark." They sat for a bit, watching people come and go before Gail spoke again. "I'm not sure what Gabe's problem is where you're concerned, but I'm sorry he's being such a pain in the behind."

"He thinks I'm a man-eater out to get your brother." Problem was, she couldn't totally blame him. She probably did appear to be an opportunist, at the least. But the last thing she wanted to do was hurt Cam.

"Are you?"

Delilah looked at her, unsure what to say.

"Out to get him, I mean."

"No." If she'd been free...but she wasn't. "We're not sleeping together," she said after a moment.

But, oh, God, she wanted to.

"I'm sorry, I know I'm prying. I realize this is none of my business, but he's my brother and I love him."

They all did. That was obvious. "Cam isn't interested in me that way." Which wasn't exactly true, but he didn't *want* to be interested in her and was fighting it for all he was worth. Just as she was.

Tonight had been close. Closer than they'd yet come to giving in to what they were feeling. Part of her hadn't wanted him to listen. Hadn't wanted him to stop. If he'd kissed her, she wouldn't have stopped him. And she knew, without a doubt, they'd have made love.

Gail laughed. "Oh, honey, you're wrong about that. Why else would Gabe be so bent out of shape?"

She looked at Gail and saw concern, but not condemnation in her face. "Gabe's wrong. There's nothing going on."

"It's not a crime if there is, you know."

She didn't think Gail would be so sympathetic if she knew Delilah's secrets. Gail patted her hand. "Cam's a grown man. I think he's old enough and wise enough to know what he's doing. So if he trusts you, why shouldn't I?"

"Gabe doesn't."

She looked at her brother with a worried frown. "I know. Like I said, I'm not sure what that's about." She got up and rubbed her neck, glancing at the doors worriedly. "I wonder why someone doesn't come tell us something? I'd kill for a cup of coffee."

"Let me get it," Delilah said, glad for something useful to do. "I'll bring some for everyone."

After asking at the information desk, she went downstairs to the cafeteria to the coffee machine.

She filled one cup and turned around to look for a container to hold several more. There was a man with his back to her at one of the machines on the opposite wall. A man with brown hair with a glint of silver. Wearing an overcoat just like Avery Freeman's.

She choked on a scream and dropped the coffee, hardly noticing the hot liquid splashing on her jeans and tennis shoes. How had he found her?

The man turned around, the annoyance on his face fading when he saw her. "Are you all right?"

She stared at him, unable to speak. Not Avery, was all she could think. Dizzy, she sucked in a deep breath. It wasn't him. Thank God, it wasn't him.

"Miss, are you all right?" he repeated, and handed her some paper napkins.

"Fine. Sorry. I'm—clumsy." She felt as if her tongue were sticking to the roof of her mouth. She knew she sounded and looked like an idiot, but her hands were trembling so badly from her fright, she couldn't do anything about that.

He looked doubtful but left after she reassured him she was fine. Delilah sank down near the machine, hanging her head and fighting to gain control. She had to get out of there. Go somewhere Avery wouldn't find her. Somewhere safe.

CHAPTER THIRTEEN

CAM WALKED INTO THE APARTMENT and threw his keys down on the table by the door. In the muted light thrown by the television, he could barely make out Delilah, huddled on the sofa with a blanket wrapped around her.

"What the hell happened to you? Gail said you went to get coffee and never came back."

"I'm sorry. I had to leave." Her voice was flat and emotionless. Hesitant, as if she were having a hard time speaking.

Baffled, he looked at her. Wasn't she even going to ask him about his mother? She didn't, so he sat on the couch and said, "They sent my mother home. It was indigestion, not a heart attack. She was embarrassed to make such a big deal of it, but Jay said that happens all the time."

For a long moment she still didn't speak. Finally, she said, "I'm glad she's all right."

Something was off. She was acting like she was

in shock. "Did Gabe say something to upset you? Gail said he'd been giving you a hard time. Is that why you left?"

Her laugh held no humor. "It wasn't Gabe."

He started to get annoyed again. "So you just ran out for no reason. Didn't it occur to you that I—that Gail might be worried when you disappeared like you did?"

"I had a reason." She shuddered and pulled the blanket tighter around her. "I was scared."

The annoyance faded, replaced by concern. She sounded like she was fighting tears. He hated when women cried, especially when they were trying not to. You'd think he'd be used to it, and he was, but he didn't like it. He put his arm around her and pulled her close, rubbing his hand up and down her arm where the blanket had slipped down. Her skin felt chilled. She really was upset.

"It's okay. What are you scared of? Tell me what happened."

Her body tensed, her back went rigid. "I thought I saw Avery."

Avery. She'd finally said his name. Not because she trusted him, though. Because she was too upset to realize she'd let it slip. "The guy you've been running from."

She nodded. "It wasn't him, but I thought it was. I panicked. I had to get out of there."

"You've made him into some kind of superhuman bogeyman. What do you think he's going to do? Come snatch you without anyone knowing? Without anyone lifting a finger to help you? Without *you* stopping him?"

"He might. You don't know him," she said, but her body relaxed into the curve of his arm.

"Delilah, look at me." He waited until she did, then said deliberately, "You're safe here. If you're so worried about this guy, we can get a restraining order."

"Say that again," she whispered, her eyes locked on his.

"We'll get a restraining order."

She shook her head. "The first part."

All he could do was try to reassure her. "You're safe here, Delilah. I promise."

She was still gazing at him, her eyes dark and big in her face. The fear had faded from her eyes and in its place was—desire. No, wrong. He had to be wrong. He was projecting what he felt onto her— to what he saw in her eyes.

On the way home tonight, once he'd had time to think of something beyond his mother, he'd realized how close he'd come to making a huge mistake. Because if he'd kissed her, he'd have made love to her. And once he did that…he wouldn't be able to have her and then forget her as he'd done with the other women since Janine. No, Delilah would be—she already was—unforgettable. And the pure hell of it was, he didn't know how much longer he was going to be able to resist her.

"If you keep looking at me that way—"

She took his face in her hands and kissed him. And he was lost. Because, God help him, he kissed her back.

Her lips were soft, and unbelievably tempting. She tasted sweet. And packed a punch stronger than any whiskey he'd ever had. Her tongue slid over his lips, into his mouth. Thrust, withdrew, repeated the motion, in a slow, sexy pace.

Just a taste, he thought. One taste. A man could only resist so much. Her tongue swept his mouth and he deepened the kiss. He met her tongue with his and pulled back, luring hers to come after his. Not thinking, but feeling. How right she felt in his arms, how good it felt to hold her, kiss her. How much he wanted her, wanted more.

She moaned, threw the blanket off, wrapped her arms around his neck and pressed closer to him, her soft unfettered breasts nestled against his chest.

He realized she wore only the T-shirt she slept in. His mind clouded and he didn't think at all as he leaned back and she followed, until he lay stretched out on the couch with Delilah on top of him. Every inch of that delicious little body touching his. He went from aroused to as hard as granite in the space of seconds when she raised herself up and straddled him, pressing her hips against his.

He knew what she wore beneath that shirt. A tiny pair of pink thong panties. Or maybe red. Or one of the bikinis, lacy wisps of nothing, that she'd bought at the store. He'd seen them often enough in his bathroom when she washed them out. And had fantasized about taking them off her, and what would happen afterward.

He put his hands on her hips and groaned when he felt the soft, bare skin of her bottom. This had to stop. This wasn't just a taste. In about thirty-seven seconds he was going to strip those panties off and plunge inside her, make love to her like he'd dreamed of doing since he'd met her.

Desperate for control, he turned his head. "Delilah, wait."

"Why?" she whispered with a slow revolution of her hips as she bent to touch her lips to his. To slip her tongue inside his mouth and drive him halfway over the edge.

He closed his eyes. He was having a really hard time remembering why making love to Delilah was such a bad idea.

"Don't talk. Don't think." She leaned down again, her mouth so close to his, he felt her soft, warm breath flutter across his lips. "Kiss me," she said huskily, "and we'll both forget."

And there was the answer. She wanted to forget. She was scared and vulnerable, and she would regret making love with him in the morning, if not before that. Too bad he regretted what he had to do right now. Because Cam didn't take advantage of vulnerable women. When he took a woman to bed it was because she damn sure wanted to be there, not because she was trying to exorcise a bad experience.

"Delilah—" He groaned as she kissed him again. Cupped her cheeks to get her attention. "If we don't stop, we're going to make love. Are you sure that's what you want?"

She stared at him, her eyes dazed and confused. He saw awareness dawn slowly as a flush spread from her face to her chest. "I—I don't—Oh, God, I'm sorry. I shouldn't have—" She rolled off him, scrambled to her feet. With one last whispered, "I'm sorry," she fled the room.

He put his arm over his eyes and swore, long and viciously. Cursed himself for being so stupidly noble. He thought of what she'd looked like just before he'd made her realize what was happening. What she clearly didn't want to happen or she wouldn't have run out.

Her image was burned in his mind. Her swollen lips, slumberous eyes. That alluring, sweet little body. Damn it, why did he have to have a conscience? Why couldn't he have just taken what she offered with no thought of the consequences?

DELILAH PRESSED HER HANDS to her flaming cheeks, her back against the closed bedroom door. What was the matter with her? How could she have done that? She'd thrown herself at Cam. If he hadn't stopped her, hadn't given her a moment to think, she'd have made love to him. And she wasn't free to do it.

Unable to even consider going to bed, she paced the room. It didn't matter if Cam made her feel wanted. If he made her feel safe. It didn't matter that she'd fallen in love with him. If she wanted him more than she'd ever wanted a man. She wasn't free and she wasn't likely to be free. Ever.

She rubbed her temples. The episode at the hospital had really shaken her. She'd tried to tell herself she'd overreacted and Avery had simply written her off, as he would a bad investment. But she knew he hadn't. Knew in her heart that Avery Freeman wasn't through with her. Would never be through with her. Not until he had her back in his power. Or dead.

Delilah didn't want to think about Avery, ever again. She wanted a new life, right here in Aransas City. But that life was never going to include being with Cam. That life would never include being able to tell him she'd fallen in love with him.

He'd kissed her like a fantasy come to life. It had felt wonderful. And right. How could anything that felt so right be so wrong?

THE NEXT DAY, Cam and Delilah avoided each other by mutual, if silent, agreement. He went off before lunch, leaving her and Martha in charge. Delilah could only hope that by the time he came back she'd have thought of a way to deal with what had happened. Maybe pretending nothing had was the best solution.

Fat chance. She couldn't look at him without remembering what it felt like to be in his arms.

Later that afternoon after the lunch crowd had cleared out, Delilah went to work on the orders. The forms were on Cam's computer, in his office. Problem was, she didn't know enough about his customer base to be sure what to order. And she couldn't locate the previous orders, which should have been on the computer, but weren't.

She thought about asking Martha for help, but then remembered Martha's confession that she was computer-phobic and how much it irritated Cam if she tried to mess with the computer. She invariably deleted files she shouldn't and after she crashed his computer, Cam had forbidden her to touch it. The only computer he would let Martha near was the one in the cash register, and she admitted it had taken him three months to teach her to work that one. Computers and Martha obviously didn't mix. If they had, he'd have had Martha doing payroll long before he gave it over to Delilah.

Cam opened the door, stopping short when he saw her at the desk. "I didn't know you were here."

"Sorry. Do you want me to leave?" She didn't have to look at him. Just the sound of his voice triggered memories of the night before.

"No, of course not." He came in and shut the door. "What are you doing?"

All right. If he could pretend, so could she. She scrolled down the screen. "I thought I'd try to fill out the liquor order, but all I could find were the forms, not the past orders. I'm not sure how much of what to ask for."

He crossed the room to the file cabinet standing

in the corner, opened a drawer and pulled out a manila folder. "I keep the last couple of orders in here. I print out a paper copy in case they get the delivery wrong. The rest of them should be on the computer."

She looked at the screen. "They should be, but I couldn't find them there. What do you file them under?"

He came to the desk and leaned over, taking the mouse from her. "I can't remember the name. I have to look."

"Under something original like 'orders'?" she asked.

He slanted her a dirty look. "Paperwork isn't my favorite thing to do. Besides, I don't really need to look at the paperwork, I know what stock I'm running low on. Ordinarily I'm the one who does this."

His head was close to hers. She gave up all pretense of looking at the screen and watched his profile instead. He found what he was searching for a few minutes later, pointing the mouse and clicking open the file labeled Miscellaneous. "There they are. Perfectly logical."

Delilah tilted her head to study him. "Logical? Miscellaneous could mean anything. Why didn't you just put it under liquor orders?"

"Too much trouble." He shrugged. "Like Cat says, I need a secretary. Want to apply for the job?"

"I already have one. Don't I?"

Their gazes locked. His eyes darkened to charcoal gray. Cam leaned closer to her as she shifted closer to him. He drew back abruptly. "I've got… something to take care of." He turned on his heel and left the room.

They couldn't avoid each other forever. Come closing time they'd be alone again. But it didn't matter. Nothing could happen. She couldn't make that mistake again.

Cam didn't seem to have a problem putting her out of his mind. He hardly spoke to her all evening. Until her run-in with the pervert.

Delilah didn't always work the bar tables, but that evening the cocktail waitress had gone home sick, so Delilah split the bar customers with Martha. She didn't pay much attention the first three times the guy tried to pick her up. You couldn't be a waitress for several years and not know how to discourage overenthusiastic patrons. But this guy wouldn't give up and he wouldn't leave either. The longer the evening went on, the drunker he got. And the more obnoxious.

So obnoxious she actually mentioned it to Martha. Martha glanced at him and shrugged. "He's not a regular. Why don't you tell Cam about it? He'll take care of him."

Right. She glanced over at him, at the busty blonde who'd been hanging all over him all night long. Like hell she'd tell him. She'd handle it herself.

Since the busboy hadn't shown either, the waitresses had to clear the tables as well. She was busing the table next to the would-be Romeo when she felt a hard pinch on her butt. Startled, she turned around to stare at the man incredulously. That hadn't been a flirtatious pat, which she didn't like but could deal with. No, that had felt more like an assault than a simple getting out of line.

Grinning at her, he said something that topped every one of his increasingly crude come-ons.

Fed up, she dumped a glass of ice water on his head. "Hands off."

He jumped up with a roar of anger, grabbing her arm. Before she could do more than jerk out of his grasp, Cam was beside them. "You're out of here," Cam told him, twisting the man's arm behind his back.

"What the hell do you mean, I'm out? That bitch dumped water on me! I didn't do anything!"

"Tell it to the cops," Cam advised him. The man sputtered, cursing her and Cam, but Cam marched him outside so quickly Delilah didn't think most of the remaining customers even knew anything had happened. Except for the blonde Cam had left. She didn't look too happy.

A short time later Cam came back in. His jaw was clenched hard and his eyes were sharp and angry. He had an incipient bruise on his cheekbone, she realized guiltily. "Delilah, my office."

She followed him in there, wishing she'd handled things differently. "I'm sorry," she said when he shut the door. "I don't usually react like that but he surprised me."

"He won't be back." He shoved a hand through his hair and she noticed blood.

"You're hurt, let me see." She grabbed his hand. "You're bleeding."

He glanced at his hand, then pulled it away and rubbed it on his jeans. "Not me. Him. I had Martha call the cops. I wasn't letting him get away with what he did to you. Or drive, either. I let go of him when they got here and he pasted me one. My stupidity for letting him go."

"So you hit him back."

He shot her an exasperated glance. "What did you want me to do, kiss him?"

"I'm sorry. I didn't mean to cause a mess."

He brushed her apology aside. "You need to find a better way to handle guys like that in the future."

His eyes flashed and she could see he was barely hanging on to his temper.

Until then, she'd been feeling guilty for blowing it but that comment sparked her own temper. "Most men don't assault the waitress," she returned hotly. "It's not like I stuck my butt out there asking for him to pinch the hell out of it. He did that with absolutely zero encouragement from me."

Cam didn't look sympathetic, he still looked angry. "I didn't say you encouraged him. I said you needed to handle it differently. Next time, call me if you have a problem." He didn't wait for an answer but left the office.

She kicked the chair and swore when it hurt her foot. Knowing he was right only made her mood worse.

Martha came up to her later that evening, ready to gossip. "What's up with Cam?"

"You mean him and the bimbo?" The blonde was still there, still hanging on every word Cam spoke to her. It shouldn't bother her that he'd spent the evening—when he hadn't been yelling at her or getting rid of perverts—flirting with the woman until Delilah was nauseated.

Martha snorted a laugh. "That one's been after him for weeks. I thought after you came he'd seen the light, but I guess not."

"Seen the light?"

"About those women and how worthless they are." She picked up four setups and poured out four waters. "The stories I could tell you." She shook her head in disgust. "I wonder about women nowadays, I really do."

"He doesn't seem to think she's worthless," Delilah said glumly, watching her put her hand on Cam's arm and stroke it possessively, her long red nails gleaming even from this distance. It didn't help one bit knowing she had no right to be jealous. No right at all.

"I wouldn't worry about it too much," Martha said, eyeing the two critically. "Cam's just passing the time."

"He looks like he's having a hell of a good time while he's at it."

Martha cut her a sly glance. "Honey, it's you he's interested in. And I'd say that goes both ways."

"Martha, it's not like that. Cam's just—" She made the mistake of looking at him again, and couldn't help wincing when the woman laughed and leaned forward, giving him a bird's-eye view of a spectacular cleavage. "We're friends, nothing more," she said flatly.

Martha picked up her tray to take it to her table. "Uh-huh. Then why does he look at you every time he thinks you're not looking and why do you look at him every time you think he's not looking?" She arched an eyebrow and, when Delilah didn't answer, continued, "And then there was that little scene earlier, when Cam threw out that drunk."

Delilah shrugged and picked up her own tray. "I can't imagine he's never had to throw out a drunk before."

Martha nodded. "Sure he has. A man was bothering Rachel not too long ago and Cam gave him the boot." She paused and added, "But all he did was toss that guy out on his can. And sweetie, there was murder in his eyes when he got rid of the one who put his hands on you. He sure didn't look that way when it was Rachel."

Martha didn't wait for an answer, but took her tray and sailed off.

Cam *had* been upset. Maybe he had yelled at her to hide his true feelings. It was a nice theory, Delilah admitted. One she held on to right up until the moment Cameron left the bar with the blonde, leaving her and Martha to close up.

CHAPTER FOURTEEN

EVERYTHING WAS DARK when Cam came home that night. He didn't bother to turn on a light in the kitchen. He knew what he wanted and where it was. He went to the cabinet, opened it, pulled out the whiskey bottle and grabbed a glass. Then he walked into the living room, sat on the couch, flipped on the television, muted it, and poured a stiff two fingers of whiskey into the glass.

Face it, he thought as he downed the liquid and it burned its way to his belly. *You're screwed. You can't make it with a woman you don't want, and you sure as hell can't make it with the woman you want.*

He knew Delilah wanted him. He could see it in her eyes, he could hear it in her voice. He'd felt it when she'd kissed him, when they had come so close to making love. She wanted him as much as he wanted her. Yet the fact remained that she'd run like hell. Each and every time they'd come close, she had run.

He knew why he kept backing off, but why did she? He scrubbed a hand over his face. Because she didn't trust him. Because she'd just escaped an abusive relationship and simply wasn't ready to trust a man again. Last night had been about comfort and forgetting. That was all.

Tonight had been about sex. He'd wanted sex without strings, without emotion clouding his mind, without meaning. Because emotion meant pain and he'd had enough of that to last him a lifetime. He'd gone home with Isabel fully intending to take her to bed. She knew the score as well as he did and she wouldn't have expected anything more than a one-night stand.

Had he ended the evening having steamy, meaningless sex in a very hot blonde's arms, and finally, finally getting some relief from the ever-present ache he'd lived with night and day since Delilah had come to town? No, of course not. That would have been too easy. Instead, he'd left the woman barely fifteen minutes after he'd arrived at her place. He'd hardly even kissed her, for crying out loud. His heart wasn't in it. Neither was anything else. He spent the next hour driving around and walking on the beach until he'd been sure Delilah would be asleep.

He drained the whiskey and slapped the glass down. Imagine that, liquor wasn't helping. Nothing was going to make him forget Delilah and what having her in his arms had felt like. Nothing short of a complete memory loss.

"That's not the face of a man who got lucky tonight," Delilah said from the doorway.

Damn it, she should have been asleep hours ago. He looked at her and wished he hadn't. She wore a long baby-blue T-shirt, one she'd borrowed from him, that hit her mid-thigh. And that was all.

He must have been an ax murderer in another life. Otherwise, why was he being tortured for trying to do the right thing?

"Go back to bed, Delilah. I'm not in the mood for small talk."

She ignored him, walked over and sat beside him. Picked up the empty glass and said, "Can I have some of that or aren't you sharing, either?"

He gritted his teeth and splashed the dark amber liquid into the glass. Caught her scent and his stomach clenched. How the hell did a woman who'd arrived on his doorstep with only a backpack manage to smell like that? Innocence and sin mixed up in one tidy package.

He watched her throat as the whiskey went down. He didn't want to, knew it was a mistake but he couldn't help it. Soft skin, he knew. Skin that begged to be touched. Kissed. His gaze fell to her breasts, full and unbound. Her nipples showed through the thin fabric. He wanted to touch her, cup those sweet breasts in his hands, taste her, like he hadn't the night before. He wanted to see her, all of her, naked and beautiful in his bed. Sweat popped out on his forehead. He forced his gaze to return to the television.

"What are you doing up?" he asked.

"I couldn't sleep. I kept…thinking."

He started to touch her, but didn't. That way lay madness. "Are you still obsessing over that guy? I told you, you're safe here."

She laughed humorlessly and put the nearly empty glass on the table. "I'm not safe anywhere while he's still alive."

"Do you wish you'd killed him, then?"

She shook her head. "No. Even though—" She broke off. "No, I don't wish I'd killed him. I couldn't handle killing a man. Even a man like him. But I wish I'd never met him. God, do I wish that."

He couldn't think of a reply to that. He splashed more liquid into his glass, then shrugged when he saw her watching him and gave it to her.

She swirled the whiskey around, then took another drink. He willed himself to ignore her. Ignore the heat, the scent, the need. Ignore the images from the night before that bombarded his mind. Images of Delilah, her face alive with passion.

"I wasn't thinking about him." She looked at him. "I was thinking about you. And me. I can't stop thinking about what happened between us."

Oh, shit. Wordlessly, Cam took the glass from her and drank some more. He had a feeling he knew what was coming.

"You can't forget last night either, can you?"

And he'd been right, damn it. "Last night?" He forced a laugh. Looked at her and smiled. "Baby, I forgot it thirty seconds after it happened."

"I don't think so," she said softly. "I think you left with that woman because you were trying to forget. You were trying to pretend that there's nothing between us."

He lifted a shoulder. "I left with her because I wanted to get laid," he said, choosing the crude words purposely. "Last time I checked that was none of your damn business."

"I know it's not. Don't you think I realize that?" Her voice was low and she didn't look at him. "I've been sitting here for the last two hours, trying not to think about you…and her. Trying not to imagine you making love to her."

She raised her eyes and met his. "Trying not to wish it was me you'd gone home with, me you were making love with."

He didn't speak. But he took a step nearer the cliff.

She moved nearer to him. Put her hand on his chest and leaned in close. So close he could feel her heat, so close he was surrounded by her scent.

"Tell me," she said quietly.

He didn't answer.

"Did you sleep with her, Cam?"

Lie, he told himself as he looked into her eyes. One lousy lie and it will be over. She was dangerous, far too dangerous for him. He couldn't risk what she made him feel. Couldn't risk falling in love with her.

But he'd been risking everything from the moment he saw her. And she wanted him. He searched her eyes, looking for doubt. He didn't find it.

"No, I didn't take her to bed," he said and fell.

She leaned closer still. "Why not?" she whispered.

"I didn't want her." He gripped her arms, stared into her eyes. "I want you, Delilah. And you know it. I want you so much it's eating me alive."

His defenses were crumbling, along with his resolve. "Once I kiss you I won't stop. Not this time. Not until I'm inside you. Hell, not then, either." He was giving her a chance to back out. A chance to come to her senses. Because he knew that once he tasted her again, he wouldn't stop until he'd had her. Until he'd tasted every inch of her, and more.

She didn't speak but reached down for the hem of her T-shirt and drew it up slowly, over her belly, her breasts, then her head. Tossed it aside. All she wore was a tiny pair of pink thong panties, the ones he'd dreamed of taking off her last night.

"Touch me," she said, her voice like a siren's.

He took her hands, carried each one to his lips. "Be sure, Delilah."

"I'm sure," she said, and placed one of his hands on her breast.

Her skin was soft, warm and alive. Her breasts were every bit as beautiful as he'd imagined, firm and full with pale rose nipples and milky skin. He cupped her breast, caressed it, slid his fingers over her nipple and watched it pearl. He was living a dream. A beautiful, erotic dream.

"You are so unbelievably beautiful."

She laughed, then her breath caught as he cupped her other breast and massaged it gently. She leaned forward and kissed him, slid her tongue into his mouth and teased him. "Take your shirt off," she said after a long, wet kiss. "I want to touch you. To feel you."

He didn't want to stop touching her long enough to do it, but the thought of that soft fragrant skin against his own bare chest was too much to resist. She helped him, their fingers meeting at the buttons. Then she lay back on the couch, parted her legs and held out her arms. He slipped between her legs, his erection snug against the damp silk of her panties. He kissed her, pushing gently against her, until her legs wrapped around him and she urged him to be faster. Harder. If he didn't get her naked soon, it was all going to be over. He wouldn't last long, not with Delilah so warm and willing in his arms.

Their lips met, clung, parted. She slicked her tongue slowly over his lips, dipped it inside his mouth, whispered, "Cam, I want you. So much."

"The bedroom." He took her mouth, hungrily, greedily, wondering if he could wait that long.

"Here. Now."

She punctuated her words by an upward thrust of her hips. A bump and grind he thought might just kill him.

Delilah was running her hands over his back and chest, then lower. Stroking him, cupping him through the denim. "Take your jeans off," she said, her voice husky.

He stood and started unbuttoning and unzipping. She hooked her fingers in her panties, ready to slip them off. "Don't," he told her, catching her hand. "Let me. I've been thinking of getting you out of those for weeks."

She stopped, looking pleased. "Really? You didn't act like it."

"But I thought it." He finished taking his jeans and briefs off and leaned down to slide the panties slowly down her legs. "Every night. Every day, too." He sat beside her, cupped her, eased a finger inside her and watched her eyes go blurry as he bent to kiss her mouth. She was hot, wet, inviting. As ready as he was.

He wanted it to last, wanted to make it good for her. He stroked, caressed, pushed her higher until she trembled on the brink of orgasm, ready to explode any moment.

It was a miracle he managed to get the condom on before he plunged inside her. Hot. Tight. She felt so good. Their eyes met and they both groaned.

"Yes," she whispered. Her legs tightened as he thrust once, twice. Again. Pushing inside and withdrawing until they were both slick with sweat and panting. She lifted her hips with each thrust, straining to meet him, matching his passion with hers until his heart nearly burst in his chest. He kissed her lips, groaned her name and came as she shattered around him.

DELILAH HAD AWAKENED in the night, wrapped in Cam's arms. His hands at her breasts, cupping them, stroking them. She'd thought about telling him, known she should. Even opened her mouth to tell him to stop, that they needed to talk. But she didn't. She couldn't. She couldn't ruin it, not yet. She wanted this night, and she took it, knowing there wouldn't be another. Couldn't be another. He kissed her, his hands slid lower…and she was lost.

But now it was morning. She had to face what she'd done in the cold light of day. And she had to tell Cam the truth. She raised up on her elbow to prop her head in her hand and look down at him, tracing her fingers over the stubble on his jaw. Lord, he was a good-looking man. And a good man. A decent man. A man she wished with all her heart could be hers.

His eyes opened, he blinked sleepily, then smiled, a slow, wicked smile.

Her heart fluttered. If only… "We need to talk," she said.

"Later," he said, drawing her down into his arms and kissing her lingeringly.

"Cam, wait," she said, turning her head. "We have to talk. Now."

His smile faded. "What's wrong?"

The doorbell rang before she could begin.

Cam sat up and shoved a hand through his hair. "Damn it, I bet that's Gabe. I forgot he was coming over this morning." He glanced at the clock. "For once he's on time. Why now?"

Great. His brother who hated her. Cam must have read her thoughts because he said, "He's not a bad guy. A little pigheaded maybe."

"I didn't say anything."

"You didn't need to. Your face said it all." Cameron grinned. "Don't worry. He'll come around when he gets to know you." He kissed her lightly, then let her go.

No, he wouldn't. He'd hate her even more when he heard what she was going to tell Cam. "Are you going to tell him about us?"

He got up, pulled on his jeans, looked at her over his shoulder. "I doubt I'll need to. However pigheaded he is, he's not stupid."

Her nerves were jumping when she walked into the kitchen half an hour later. She'd showered, dressed, even put on makeup in an attempt to bolster her courage. She straightened her back, squared her shoulders. She'd faced worse than Gabe and survived. Facing Cam later would be worse. Much worse.

Delilah greeted Gabe and went to the stove. "Let me do that," she told Cam, who was scrambling eggs.

"Thanks." He handed her the utensil and smiled, an intimate smile that told her he was thinking of the night before and not breakfast. She couldn't help smiling back.

And damn it, Gabe must have seen it, too.

"You're sleeping with her. I should have known all those protests were complete bullshit. Hell, I did know it." His tone was bitter. Angry.

He glared at Delilah as if he wanted to squash her like a bug. Then he turned to Cam. "Are you out of your freaking mind?"

Delilah pulled the pan off the fire and spooned eggs onto three plates. Not that she figured anybody would eat them. Gabe apparently had a lot of mad stored up.

"Are you nuts?" Gabe got up and strode over to Cam, getting right in his face. "Did your fortieth birthday fry your brain?"

"Butt out," Cam said. "I know what I'm doing."

"Oh, yeah. Right. She's playing you like a sailfish, bro, and you're just tail walking on the water, too dumb to even realize you're hooked." He looked Delilah up and down and sneered. "I know her type. And so should you."

"I do know her. And she's not what you're thinking."

Gabe transferred his gaze to Cam. "She's the type who takes a man for everything he's worth and after he's all used up, she walks out."

"That's enough, Gabe."

She could see his fists clench and knew he was

barely hanging on to his temper. She just wanted it to be over and Gabe gone.

But Gabe wasn't through. His eyes were angry and flinty-hard when he spoke to her. "Cam might be blinded by his do-gooder complex, but baby, I don't have one." He jabbed a finger at her, not quite touching her. "You have trouble written all over you and I don't want my brother in the middle of it when it finds you."

He turned to Cam. "You're not thinking with your brain. You're thinking with your—"

"Shut up, Gabe." Cam put a hand on her shoulder, squeezing gently. "I told you to butt out. I meant it."

Gabe looked from one to the other, his face grim. "Ten bucks says she's out of here the minute she finds a more likely mark. And you'll be damn lucky if she hasn't taken you for everything you have before she walks."

Cam shook his head. "You're way off base, Gabe. You don't know Delilah."

Gabe pulled out his wallet, tossed a crumpled ten-dollar bill on the counter. "Back it up with money."

Their eyes met but neither spoke. Delilah knew something more was going on. The tension alone was thick enough to cut with a knife.

Cam stared at the money, then looked at his brother. "You don't want to do this, Gabe."

"Match it. Unless you're not as sure of her as you say you are."

Cameron said nothing. Almost casually, he took out his own wallet and pulled out a ten-dollar bill. He laid it on the counter beside Gabe's. "You're on, Gabriel."

She didn't understand what was happening but she knew it was more than a simple bet. She couldn't stand it any longer, couldn't stand causing more problems between Cam and his brother. "Don't."

Cam looked at her. "Don't take the bet?"

She shook her head. "Gabe's right. Not that I'm after your money, but he's right about me. I've been lying to you, Cam."

CHAPTER FIFTEEN

THERE WAS A LONG, intense silence. Cam heard Gabe curse but right now he wasn't concerned with his brother. He wanted to know what Delilah meant.

"Lying about what?" he asked her. She looked sick. As sick as he was beginning to feel.

"Can we do this alone?" She looked at Gabe. "Would you—would you leave us alone, Gabe? Please."

He looked at Cam, shook his head, then walked out the door without saying another word.

"I tried to tell you this morning," Delilah said, "before Gabe came over."

He hadn't had talking on his mind. In a detached way, he noticed she was twisting her hands together nervously. "What did you lie about?" he repeated.

"When I let you think I was running from my boyfriend." She hesitated, looked at him, her eyes dark, midnight blue and swimming with tears.

He knew then. The sick feeling in his gut told

him. But he asked anyway. "He's not your boy-friend, is he?"

She shook her head, her eyes still locked on his. "He's my husband."

Her words hit him like a nuclear blast. *She's mar-ried* was all he could think. *Goddamn it, she lied to me.* "You didn't think I needed to know that before I had sex with you?"

"I didn't think—I didn't mean for it to happen."

"That's something we can sure as hell agree on." He turned away, then back to look at her. "Stop look-ing at me like that. Do you think I'm going to hit you?"

"Avery did," she said simply.

"Yeah, well, unlike him I don't hit women." He knew it was mean, but he didn't care. He wanted her to hurt as much as he did. "I asked you straight out and you told me you weren't married."

"I was afraid. I didn't know you and I was terri-fied of what would happen if he found me. I had no-where else to go. It just seemed better to not tell you."

"And later, after you knew me? You couldn't tell me the truth then? You couldn't tell me before I—" He stopped, furious. Goddamn it, why hadn't she told him before he'd made love to her? Before he'd fallen in love with her.

She shook her head. "I should have. After that night, when I thought I'd seen Avery…"

The night he'd first kissed her.

"I promised myself nothing more would happen between us. And I meant it. I swore I wouldn't… But it was too late."

"So is this like a game to you? To make me crazy with wanting you until I can't take it anymore and then once I finally make love to you, boom, you tell me you've been lying to me? What a kick that must have been."

"No!" She started toward him, her hand outstretched. "How can you think that?"

He backed up and held up his hand. "You don't want to touch me right now, Delilah. Just…don't."

She halted, stunned pain in her gaze. "Cam, last night meant more to me than you can possibly imagine, and I'm not sorry it happened. Because it's the most beautiful thing that ever happened to me."

He'd done it again. Trusted a woman and been slammed in the teeth. "How stupid, how gullible do you think I am? Do you think because Janine made a fool of me that I'll swallow any garbage you care to spill?"

She shook her head, a trail of tears tracking her cheeks. "I'm sorry I hurt you. Sorry I didn't tell you. You have every reason, every right to hate me."

"Damn you," he said, and walked out. Hate her? He wished he could. She was a liar. She was married. And he was in love with her.

SHE'D GOTTEN NO MORE than she'd deserved, she knew. His utter contempt for her. Well, he couldn't possibly think worse of her than she did herself. She had to leave. Cam wouldn't want her there, not after she'd lied so disastrously. But even if he'd be willing for her to stay, she couldn't stand seeing him day after day knowing he hated her. Knowing she loved him and that any kind of a future between them was doomed.

It didn't take long to pack. Even with having to stop because she was crying too hard to see. She didn't have much. And she couldn't take anything with her that Cam or his family had given her.

She slung her backpack over her shoulder. Straightened and wiped her eyes. She could cry later. Right now she had to tell Cam goodbye. She owed him that, and her thanks for everything he'd done for her.

She turned around and saw him standing in the doorway. Her heart stuttered as she realized this might be her last image of him. He looked tired. And angry. And beneath it all, she could see the pain in his eyes. The pain and misery she'd put there.

"Running away again?"

"I didn't think you'd want me here."

He didn't respond to that. He walked into her room, stood gazing at her, his face blank. "Was it all a lie?"

"Last night wasn't a lie. I wanted you." I love you, she thought, but didn't say. He wouldn't believe her. "I needed you." She still did, even though she would never have him.

Anger flickered again in the depths of his eyes, turning them almost black. "If you're smart, you won't talk about last night," he said harshly. "Is the rest of it true? Did your husband beat you?"

"Yes."

"Did he choke you? Drug you? Lock you up?"

"Yes." She raised her chin and gazed at him. "Do you believe me?"

His expression was bleak now. He sat down, heavily, on her bed. "Yeah. Damn it, I do."

Not much, but it might be more than she deserved. "Will you let me tell you about it? Why I married him and why I knew I had to get away?"

"That depends." He looked at her now, his expression hard and unforgiving. "On how much is going to be truth and how much of what you're telling me will be bullshit."

"Why don't you decide that after I've told you?"

She met his gaze, striving for, if not dignity, at least composure.

Impassively, he folded his arms over his chest. "Have at it."

She drew in a deep breath and spoke his full name for the first time since she'd left him. "His name is Avery Freeman. He's a corporate attorney in Houston. Well-respected, wealthy. With connections everywhere but especially in the police department." She gave a short, unamused laugh. "He's everything I'm not."

Cam didn't speak. She couldn't read his expression, which was probably just as well. She went on, finding a surprising relief in telling the whole story, regardless of the fact that her audience doubted every word out of her mouth.

"I was a waitress at a steak place in Houston. Not the fanciest place in town, but not a dive either. Sometimes I worked the bar. The tips were good." She smiled wryly. "Especially if you wore a short skirt. I needed every penny I could get to go to school part-time. Accounting, like I told you before. I did a little bookkeeping on the side. I was making it, but it wasn't easy.

"There was a guy who started coming in regularly, and he always tried to sit at one of my tables. The others teased me about it, since he'd wait at the bar until he could sit at my table. He tipped well, so I didn't mind. It didn't occur to me at first that he was interested in me. He was older, in his mid-forties, I thought." She paused and looked at him, waiting for a comment.

He gave her a cynical smile. "I'd already figured out you like older men."

Neither the smile nor the comment were encouraging, but at least he'd spoken. "Avery was really nice. Charming. Handsome. Respectful, which I didn't get a lot of, so that was appealing. He didn't put the moves on me, which surprised me. He talked to me. I enjoyed it. Enjoyed him."

She closed her eyes, then sat down on the other end of the bed and began again. *Just tell him. Don't think, just talk.* "He started staying later and later. After I got off work, he'd walk me to my car. Because I wouldn't let him follow me home, not at first. Like I told you, I'd been on my own for a long time, and I'd learned to be wary." She grimaced. "Not wary enough. After a while, I relented. We started dating." She faltered, fell silent.

"What is it?" he asked.

"I was trying to think why I missed the signs that should have clued me in to what he was really like. They were subtle, at first, but they were there."

"Why did you?"

She hesitated. "The only answer I have is that I wanted to believe him. So I ignored the signs. He'd take me places, fancy restaurants, even the opera, but he never, or rarely, introduced me to anyone. Not friends, not family. I think I met a total of three people he knew, the whole time I was with him. I thought he wanted me to himself. I was even…flattered." God, why hadn't she seen how odd that was? Or how controlling he was? How he'd moved in so smoothly and taken over her life. But she hadn't, whatever her reasons.

"He bought me clothes. Beautiful clothes. Jewelry. I didn't feel right taking so much from him, but he made it sound so reasonable. He'd say he loved being able to buy me things. He said he appreciated my scruples, but it wasn't a hardship for him. I knew he was wealthy, but I still resisted. He'd act so disappointed when I wouldn't let him. So after a while, I quit fighting him. I accepted whatever he gave me and I buried my qualms."

It was harder now. Harder to admit how foolish she'd been. How she'd allowed herself to be taken in by his smooth manner, his practiced lies.

"It happened so fast, he just sort of swept me along in his wake. He said he wanted to take care of me. And I was tired of being alone. Tired of struggling. He promised me all sorts of things. The thought of not having to worry about money any-more tempted me, but the emotional promises were even more appealing. He swore he loved me, and I believed him. And since I did, I let him convince me to marry him."

"Did you love him?"

She shook her head, ashamed to admit it but she had to be honest. "I wanted to. I thought I'd grow to love him, because he loved me so much. I cared about him. Or I cared about the man I thought he was. But that man was all smoke and mirrors." She gripped her hands together, bowed her head. "The real man, well, he showed me quickly enough after the wedding who that was."

"What did he do?"

She looked up at him. Was it her imagination or had the anger eased from his eyes, from his voice?

She'd come this far. Might as well tell him the whole, wretched, sordid truth. "One night I had a headache. A bad one. Avery wanted to…make love." She looked away, not wanting to see his face when she told him the rest. "I told him I didn't feel well. He—he didn't care."

"Delilah, look at me." His voice was soft, the tone gentle.

She shook her head, her throat closing. Hesitantly, he reached over and put his hand over hers.

"It's not your fault."

She looked at their hands, seeing the strength of his, how small hers looked beneath it. "I—he didn't rape me."

"He forced you to have sex against your will. What else would you call it?"

"It wasn't like that. Exactly. He said we were married and he was my husband, so I owed him my obedience." Sickened at the memory, she looked at Cam. "Obedience. As if I was a dog." She sucked in air, determined not to cry. "But I—I was afraid if I didn't—I didn't like the look in his eyes. Or the way he held me. So tight, his fingers digging into my arms… So I let him."

Cam let go of her hand and stood. "Bastard." He paced away a few steps then turned to look at her. "Being married doesn't make that right, Delilah."

She just shook her head. There was more. And it was worse, much worse than that. "The next day he acted as if nothing had happened. I did, too. I wasn't sure… God, I was so stupid. I thought maybe he'd had too much to drink and he didn't mean it. He had been drinking, but he wasn't drunk. I just pretended to myself he had been. It made it easier."

"You stayed with him."

"We'd only been married a couple of months. I wanted it to work. I thought maybe it was my fault.

That I was making it into something it wasn't. But deep down, I knew. I knew it was wrong. And I worried it would get worse. And it did.

"He didn't like my friends. Didn't want them around. So rather than making everyone uncomfortable, I quit asking them to come over. He talked me into quitting my job. He had promised before we married to help me through school. So I thought, great, I'll be able to go to school full-time."

"How did he stop you?"

"Nothing so simple as not paying for it. He got rid of my car." She smiled at his exclamation of disgust. "At first he said it was in the shop, but after a few weeks he couldn't keep that up. So he said his first wife had died in a car wreck. That she'd been drinking and had run off the road. He couldn't bear to think of me getting into an accident. His solution was for me not to drive.

"The car—that was the real wake-up call. I couldn't rationalize it, like I had the other. I knew then that I was in trouble. I'd had a friend in an abusive relationship. Her boyfriend started out with just that kind of controlling behavior. Behavior that escalated into violence. And however stupid I'd been up to that point, I'm not normally a stupid person."

"You weren't stupid, Delilah. You believed in the wrong person."

Like he had. She read the thought in his eyes, though he didn't speak it.

She drew in another breath and continued. "I could see where it was headed. I found a lawyer in the phone book and begged him to see me. He gave me an appointment the next day. I must have sounded desperate. I waited until Avery went to work the next day and I called a cab and went to see the lawyer."

"You filed for divorce?"

"No." She closed her eyes for a moment, then opened them. "I talked to the lawyer about the possibility of divorce. But then I made a huge mistake, almost worse than marrying him in the first place. I wanted to think about it. I needed to be sure before I ended my marriage, after such a short time. I went through everything, point by point. He hadn't hit me. Maybe he wouldn't. Maybe I was imagining the control issues." She lifted a shoulder. "It doesn't matter why. I went back.

"Avery was waiting for me. He asked me how my meeting with the lawyer went and mentioned him by name. He'd dialed star sixty-nine and gotten the taxi company and traced me through them. I don't know how, but I imagine he bribed somebody." She looked at Cam who was gazing at her intently. She gave a weak smile. "I never thought of that."

"You don't need to say any more. I can guess the rest. The son of a bitch beat you and drugged you. Then he locked you up." He looked grim and angry. At least this time his anger was directed at Avery.

"Yes. But that's not all."

He sat again. "Go on. Finish it."

"He went ballistic. Started screaming and cursing at me. Hitting me. He said I wasn't going to divorce him. I wasn't going to get away. I was his. His property. He *owned* me. That bitch Anita had thought she could divorce him but she'd found out different. He'd taught her respect before she died. And then he laughed and said I'd better be careful, that accidents happen all the time."

"Anita was his first wife? The one who died in a car wreck?"

"Yes. His first wife. The woman he murdered when she tried to divorce him."

Cam stared at her. Their gazes locked, she added, "And he got away with it."

CHAPTER SIXTEEN

CAM HAD THOUGHT Delilah's story couldn't get any worse. It just had. He was reeling from a dozen emotions. Anger at her. Pain over her betrayal. Rage at what the son of a bitch had done to her, and had nearly managed to do. He didn't doubt the truth of what Delilah had told him. He couldn't say why, when he knew she had lied, but every word of that chilling story held a ring of truth.

"How do you know he killed her? Did he admit it?"

She shook her head. "No, he's not that crazy. I don't have proof. Except here." She touched her chest, over her heart. "I know he killed her, Cam. And one other thing." She got up and dug through her backpack until she hauled out a small bound book and handed it to him. "This is his first wife's diary. I found it in the bedroom he locked me in."

Wondering what he'd find inside, he opened it. There was a poem on the first page. He flipped through and saw other poems, interspersed with narrative. Near the end, a title caught his eye. "Shattered Dreams." He read a little, then looked at Delilah, thoroughly shaken. It spoke of dreams and death, the death of her love. A love that had been systematically beaten out of her by her husband.

"God. How could he—what a sick bastard he is."

"She was a poet. He promised he'd help her get published. She loved him. She believed him. She was twenty-two years old, Cam, when he killed her."

"I don't know what to say." He closed the diary. "As bad as this is, it doesn't prove he killed her."

"No, it's not proof. But Cam, she didn't drink. He told me she was driving drunk and in her diary she says she couldn't drink because she was allergic to any kind of alcohol. She couldn't even drink a beer without getting sick." She took the book from him and paged to the back. "The last entry is a poem. About divorce. I think she asked him for a divorce and I think he killed her for it."

"If you believe that then why haven't you gone to the cops? Why didn't you do that right away? The minute you got out of there you should have gone to them."

"I couldn't risk him finding me. Besides, I didn't think it would matter. I told you he got away with it. The police don't suspect him."

"How do you know that?"

"When I looked online to see if he was dead…I didn't spend all my time doing that. I thought maybe I'd overreacted. Maybe he hadn't really killed her. Maybe her death really had been accidental. Just because he beat her, just because he beat me, didn't mean he'd killed her. So I looked her up. I found some articles about the accident. They all mentioned the suspicion that it was alcohol related."

"Still, Delilah—"

"I'm not finished. The car went over a cliff and exploded on impact. She was burned so badly she was hardly recognizable. I think he planned that so it would make it difficult or impossible to tell what injuries happened during the crash. And what he'd done to her before that. When he beat her to death."

Oh, God, she could be right. "You're right. When you put it all together, it's suspicious as hell. Which is why you have to go to the cops, Delilah. You can't keep this to yourself."

"I can if I want to live."

"We'll tell Maggie. The police will protect you." And he would, too. Because he knew, no matter what she'd done, that he couldn't walk away from her. He couldn't walk away and live with himself.

She laughed bitterly. "You're living in a dream world. You must not know the statistics on abused women. Even if the police believe me, they can't protect me. Once Avery finds me, there's nothing to stop him from coming up and shooting me in broad daylight if he wants."

"So your solution is what? To always be on the run? To always be afraid he'll find you?" To be tied to an abusive killer for the rest of her life. Never to be able to move on, have a fresh start. "What kind of life is that?"

"At least I have a life," she said flatly.

She sat down and buried her face in her hands. He wanted to touch her, comfort her. But beneath it all he still hurt. Still felt betrayed. He *had* been betrayed. And goddamn it, he still wanted her so much he would have sold his soul to have her.

She looked up and gazed at him, her eyes dark and brimming with emotion. "Why should they listen to me? To accuse anyone of such a thing, much less a respected attorney, takes a lot of resolution. Not to mention a faith in the system I just don't have. I've never had much luck with the police."

"You've said things like that before. What are you talking about? Have you been arrested? Charged with something?"

She nodded. "After my mother died I went a little wild. I got involved with someone several years older than me. He was bad news, but I didn't see it." She shrugged. "I don't guess I cared.

"Anyway, he boosted a car and took me joyriding. Of course, he didn't mention he'd stolen it. We were arrested and I was charged as an accomplice. If my boyfriend had had his way, I'd have been charged with worse. The judge believed me, though, and the charges were dropped." She looked at him bleakly. "Juvenile records are purged when you become an adult, but cops don't like me. I mean, look at your friend Maggie's reaction to me."

So men had been taking advantage of her since she was sixteen. He wished that didn't bother him, but it did. "Maggie hasn't heard this story. She's a good cop, Delilah. She'll help you."

"I can't." She picked up the diary and placed it in the backpack. Got up and slung the pack over her shoulder.

"You're not leaving," he said.

"You don't want me here."

"No, I don't," he said harshly. "But I'm not having your death on my conscience. You run off and God knows what will happen to you. You're as safe here as anywhere. So just save us both a lot of trouble and forget about leaving."

"If I stay we can't—we can't be together again."

He gave her a nasty smile. "Don't worry, sugar. The way I'm feeling right now, you're the last woman on earth I'd have sex with."

Which was, he knew, a goddamn lie.

GABE WAS WAITING for him when he went to the bar. Cam didn't know what to say to his brother. He wasn't up for another scene, especially not one where he had to admit just how stupid he'd been.

"You look like shit," Gabe said.

"Yeah, well I feel like it, too." He went around behind the bar and pulled out a bottle of whiskey. Reached over and picked up a shot glass and carried both around to the other side of the bar.

"It's eleven o'clock in the morning," Gabe said, watching him splash liquid into the glass.

"Yeah, so?" Thank God today was Monday and the restaurant was closed. He tossed the liquor back and refilled his glass.

"You don't do this. You always—"

Cam said something short and crude that shut Gabe up. Raised his glass and said, "If you're going to say I told you so, go ahead and do it. But don't be surprised if I punch you in the face."

Gabe grinned. "You can try if it will make you feel better." Sobering, he said, "You're really stuck on her, aren't you?"

Cam didn't speak, he just drank more. Naturally, his brother didn't give up. Cam hadn't really expected him to.

"It's not just sex, is it?"

"No. Goddamn it. It's more."

"So what's the problem? Other than the fact she lied to you, I mean?"

He looked at Gabe. "She's married."

"Oh." He added a word that perfectly expressed Cam's feelings.

Cam laughed and poured again. "Yeah. To an abusive son of a bitch," he continued. "And she can't get a divorce because she's afraid he'll kill her if he finds her." He watched Gabe when he added, "Like he killed his first wife."

"Wow." For a minute Gabe just looked at him. "Do you believe her?"

"I wish I didn't."

"But you do."

Cam nodded. "Tell me how incredibly stupid I'm being."

Gabe shook his head. "I'm not going to tell you that. If you believe her, knowing she's lied before, I've got to think you have a reason."

"I do. The son of a bitch choked her. I saw the bruises on her neck the first night she was here." He gulped more whiskey. "She had his fingerprints on her neck, Gabe. It makes me sick to think of him doing that to her."

"Damn. This sucks."

"Tell me about it."

They were both silent. Cam was starting to feel the liquor but it wasn't helping. He was pretty sure nothing would.

"You want to go fishing?" Gabe asked after awhile.

"You think fishing's the answer to everything."

"It is," his brother said.

"What the hell." He stood and picked up the bottle. "You fish. I'll drink."

"You're on," Gabe said.

DELILAH DIDN'T KNOW what else to do, so she stayed. Partly because Cam was right and she was as safe or safer than if she moved on. But mostly because she didn't want to leave Cam. She didn't want to think about never seeing him again. Not yet. She wasn't that strong.

She knew Cam had left with Gabe because she'd looked out the window and seen them getting into Gabe's truck. So whatever he was doing, at least he was with his brother. She didn't want him to be alone. And while Gabe couldn't stand her, he obviously cared about his brother.

Around ten, she heard a noise and got up to check it. It was coming from the kitchen. As she stood back in the shadows, Gabe and Cam came in the door. Gabe had his arm around Cam, supporting him, though from what she could see, Cam was trying to shove him away.

She heard Gabe say, "Just shut up," in exasperated tones. She couldn't make out Cam's mumbled reply. Not wanting them to see her, she ducked back into her room. But the brief glimpse she'd had of Cam chilled her. He looked terrible.

She heard them stumbling down the hall to Cam's room, banging into the walls a couple of times. The door slammed shut. A little while later, Gabe came out. Delilah was waiting for him. "Is he—is he all right?"

He stared at her so long she didn't think he'd answer. "He's miles from all right. He's trashed." He took a step toward her. She stood her ground, though it cost her. "I just poured him into bed."

"He's—he's been drinking?"

Gabe laughed harshly. "Yeah, he tried to crawl into a bottle to see if he could forget you. How does it feel to drive a man to drink, Delilah? You're some piece of work, you know that?" His eyes narrowed as he stared at her. "Cam doesn't get trashed. Ever."

"I'm sorry," she whispered, her throat tight with tears she couldn't shed.

"Oh, wait. I'm wrong." Gabe smiled at her cynically. "He did this one other time. When he caught his fiancée cheating on him."

There didn't seem to be anything to say to that. "He told you, didn't he." It wasn't a question. She knew he had.

"Yeah. He needed to talk to someone he could trust." He sneered the last word.

When she didn't speak, he continued, his voice growing harsher, angrier with every word he spoke. "Why did you do it? He would have helped you, no matter what. You didn't have to get him in the sack to make sure of that."

"I didn't—"

He interrupted her, ruthlessly overriding her protest. "You knew it. You couldn't have worked for him two days without knowing he helps every damn stray who comes to him. My God, all you have to do is listen to the lousy bands he lets play at the Parrot to know what he's like. Were you jerking him around for the hell of it? Were you just bored? Or—"

"Stop it!" She wanted to put her hands over her ears but it wouldn't help. She'd still hear the words. Still feel the contempt and anger. Still feel the soul sickness that she'd lied to Cam and broken his faith one more time.

"Tell me, goddamn it. Tell me why you—"

"I'm in love with him!" She fought back tears, knowing once she started crying she would break down entirely. Gabe was staring at her, and she realized that for once she'd robbed him of words.

"I love him. That's why I slept with him." Drained, empty, she looked at him. She was tired. So damn tired. "Get out of my room."

Gabe stepped back. She heard him say her name as she closed the door in his face.

CHAPTER SEVENTEEN

THE NEXT FEW DAYS were a torture Cam never wanted to repeat. He treated Delilah coldly, impersonally. Tried to pretend she was just another employee, but they both knew she wasn't. Every time he looked at her, he remembered holding her, making love to her. And he remembered the lie.

Every night he lay in bed wanting her, knowing he couldn't have her. Every morning he woke up aching for her. If he'd thought it was bad before he'd made love to her, now it was a thousand times worse.

Every night he asked himself the same question. Could he really blame her for lying? Given the circumstances, her absolute terror and certainty that Avery Freeman would kill her if he found her, he wasn't sure he could blame her.

Not at first.

But later. It always came back to the same thing. She hadn't trusted him enough to tell him the truth. Not until it was too late.

Not surprisingly, the endless loop of his emotions being at war made him bad-tempered, miserable company. He was abrupt with his staff, curt to his patrons. As for his family, with the exception of Gabe, he avoided them. Gabe already knew everything and didn't make the mistake of thinking he wanted to talk.

So Cat had sicced his brother-in-law Mark on him when he couldn't help but deal with him. At two in the afternoon on a weekday, the place was empty, and Cam was the only one working. Resigning himself, he slid a coaster in front of Mark. "Your usual?"

Mark grinned. He loved that Cam owed him free beer for life. Cam would have thought he'd let it go after a year or so, but no such luck. He didn't abuse it, he never had more than one, but once or twice a week he'd come in and make sure Cam paid up.

"No beer for me. I've got some more errands to run. Better make it iced tea."

"Lucky me," Cam said, picking up the pitcher and pouring a glass.

"Today you are. You shouldn't bet against a sure thing," Mark said with another smile, referring to the bet Cam had lost before Mark and Cat had married, the one that had netted him the free beer. "Who could resist Cat?"

"Not you, obviously," Cam said. He hadn't

trusted Mark at first but over the years they'd become good friends. Now he didn't even mind that he'd lost the bet with Gail since it meant Mark had become his brother-in-law.

"So, what's going on?" Cam asked, setting Mark's drink in front of him.

"It's like this." He took a sip of tea. "Since she and Gail both struck out, Cat's been trying for three days to pump Gabe. He's not talking. Which, since Gabe has a notoriously big mouth, is driving her bonkers. So she sent me over here. I'm supposed to be subtle and find out what's going on with you and Delilah, but I don't do subtle."

Cam frowned. The last thing he needed was his sister—either of them—hounding him. He should have known they wouldn't give up so easily. "Nothing's going on. Cat needs to butt out." He gave the bar a frustrated rub. "Why did she send you to do her dirty work?"

Mark rolled his eyes. "If you were married you wouldn't have to ask that. Come on, Cam. Cat thinks you'll talk to me because I'm a guy and not related. And if you don't, then I have to go back home and listen to my wife yammer at me."

"Not my problem. You're on your own, buddy."

"Rumor has it you have the hots for the lady in question. And that there's trouble in paradise."

"Rumor has a nasty way of being wrong. And if Martha's been talking—"

Mark laughed. "Get real, Cam. Of course, Martha's talking. You can't go to work every day with the disposition of a boa constrictor and expect her not to talk. Remember, this is Martha."

If Cam had any sense he'd fire her. But he knew he wouldn't. "Give it a rest, Mark," he said wearily. "I'm not going to talk about it."

Mark studied him for a minute. "Are you okay?"

"I'm fine," Cam said, and they both knew he was lying. He refilled Mark's tea and they started discussing the latest ball game.

Mark glanced at the door, at the man who had just walked in. "Wonder what he's doing here?"

Tall, dark hair, sharp eyes. Cam's gut tightened. He hadn't pegged him yet, but he had a feeling the man was bad news. "Who is he?"

"He's a private investigator out of Houston. Got any ideas why he'd be here?"

"No." He hoped. A P.I. from Houston. Coincidence? Maybe, but he was getting a very bad feeling.

Mark greeted the man. "Hey, Waxman. What brings you to our little slice of paradise?"

"Business." He shook hands, then took the bar stool next to Mark. "But I wouldn't mind a cold one. A draft for me," he said to Cam.

To Mark he said, "I heard you got hitched and transferred to some hole in the wall." He leaned on the bar, glancing around with a superior air that made Cam want to slug him.

"Yep, married, kids, the whole shebang."

"Better you than me," Waxman said with a laugh. "How's it been going, Mark? Long time no see."

"Can't complain. Haven't seen you since that case we worked on in Dallas. Stolen pets, remember? Gotta be six or seven years ago now."

"That'd be about right."

"Still in the detective business?"

Waxman nodded and took a drink of his beer. "What can I say, it pays the rent."

"What are you looking for this time?"

"Not what. Who." He reached into his jacket pocket and pulled out a picture, showing it to both of them as he handed it to Cam. "Either of you seen this woman anywhere?"

Mark's gaze flicked to Cam, then back to the detective. He whistled. "Never seen her. Wouldn't mind if I did, though."

He'd known who it was the instant the guy pulled out the picture. But he'd never seen this Delilah, sophisticated, smooth, sexy as sin in a short black cocktail dress with diamonds around her throat and hanging from her ears.

"Sorry." He shook his head and handed it back. "Who is she?"

"Anne Freeman, though she probably isn't going by that name. Her husband's pretty frantic." He drank some more beer, wiped his mouth. "She skipped town several weeks ago and nothing will convince him she left of her own free will. He's positive something bad is going on. Says he reported her missing the day after she disappeared, but the cops haven't found anything. He got tired of waiting, I guess."

He put the picture back in his pocket and laughed. "Personally, I think he ought to check the bank vault. Young, sexy, hungry. Those hot ones are all alike. Especially when the sizzler in question hooks up with a guy twenty years or so older than she is."

Cameron didn't say anything. He prayed Delilah wouldn't finish up in his office and come out. If he could have left without making the man suspicious he'd have gone to warn her. He pulled out a towel and polished the bar, wishing the man would leave.

"Any particular reason you came to Aransas City?" Mark asked.

"Got a tip she might be headed south, along the coast. Do you know how many two-bit, hick towns there are along the Texas coast?"

"Watch it," Mark said. "I live here and I happen to like it."

"Sorry. Well, I need to get moving. No woman, no bonus." He drained his beer and threw some bills on the counter, along with a business card. "Here's my card if you do happen to see her. My cell phone's on there. Give me a call if you're ever in Houston."

Cam waited until the door closed behind the man before speaking. "Why didn't you say anything?"

"I like Delilah," Mark said simply. "Figured Waxman showing around her photo wasn't good news." He waited a beat and added, "So, she's married?"

Cam looked at him. "Yeah. And she's afraid her husband will kill her if he finds her."

"Why doesn't she go to the police?"

"Too long of a story," Cam said. "Right now I need to go tell her about this." He turned and looked back at Mark before he left the room. "Thanks."

"No problem," Mark said.

DELILAH LOOKED UP when Cam entered the office. Since he'd been avoiding her whenever possible, she was a little surprised. Then she saw his face.

"What's wrong?" She got up and walked over to him, laying a hand on his arm. "Cam, what is it?"

"A private detective came into the bar asking about you. Freeman sent him."

The blood drained from her face. She grabbed

him, her nails digging into his arm. "A private investigator was here? In the restaurant? What did you tell him? Oh, my God, does he know I'm here?"

"What kind of bastard do you think I am? Of course I didn't tell him. Neither did Mark. No one else was there."

She dropped his arm and moved away, pacing the small office. "Oh, God, I knew this might happen but…" She covered her mouth with a shaking hand. "He'll find me. I know he will." She whirled and started for the door.

"Delilah, wait." He took her arm, restraining her. "You're safe. The PI doesn't know you're here. There's no reason for him to come back."

She could hardly think. She fought a sense of panic, knowing it wouldn't help. "Are you insane? If a private detective has gotten this far, it's only a matter of time. What if he asks around town? I have to leave. I'm not staying here like a sitting duck, waiting for Avery to find me and kill me." She jerked out of his hold and fumbled with the door. An instant later, she was out.

She ran down the hall and crashed into someone. For a minute she didn't know who it was and she smothered a scream. A man cursed and grabbed her arms. She looked up into Gabe Randolph's dark brown eyes.

God, could this day get any worse?

"Let go of me."

He ignored her struggles to free herself. "What's the matter with you? You were running out of the office like a crazy person."

"Let me go. I have to go." She thumped a fist on his chest, but he held on, impervious.

"Let her go, Gabe."

Gabe looked at Cam, then dropped her arms. She fled.

"WHAT THE HELL is going on?" Gabe asked.

"I just told her a P.I. was in here asking about her. She's freaking out."

"Yeah, I got that. Does he know anything?"

Cam shook his head. "He's checking out towns along the coast. She's safe for now."

"You'd better go convince her of that."

"I intend to," Cam said grimly.

"Wait a minute," Gabe said when Cam would have gone. "I've been watching you both the past few days. I've never seen two more miserable human beings."

"I don't have time for this, Gabe."

"You're crazy in love with her."

"And your point is? She lied—"

"Yeah, she lied," Gabe interrupted. "You remember that day you got so wasted?"

"I remember the hangover the next day. Not much else is clear."

"I talked to her that night, after I left you. I was pissed and I blasted her, let her have it with both barrels. I asked her why she'd slept with you when she must have known you'd have helped her anyway. She said she was in love with you."

"And you believed her? You? You're the one who thought she was bad news from the first."

Gabe shrugged. "Maybe I changed my mind. I don't think she was lying about that."

"Even if it's true, what the hell am I supposed to do? What difference does it make when she's too scared to do anything except take off?"

"I don't know. But if it was me, I'd try like hell to get her to go to the cops."

Gabe was right. He hadn't pushed enough before. Maybe the scare she'd just had would help change her mind. "Take care of the restaurant," Cam told him. "Martha's here. Tell her to help you."

"You know I hate that. Besides, I'm a crappy bartender."

"Tough. Deal with it."

"All right, but you owe me for this, Cam."

"I owe you for more than that," Cam said.

CHAPTER EIGHTEEN

THE SHAKES HIT HER about the time she reached her room. She had to sit on the bed until they eased. She wasn't surprised. She'd known Avery would hire a private detective. But she hadn't expected him to find her. Had prayed he wouldn't. Not here, in this out-of-the-way small town.

But he hadn't found her, she reminded herself. Not yet. It brought it home to her, though, just how easily he might have. If she'd walked into the bar…

She got up, opened the closet and dragged out her backpack. Checked the wallet for the cash she'd been hoarding. Unfortunately, it didn't take long to count. Not as much as she'd like, but more than she had the last time she ran. Enough to get by for a few weeks, if she were careful. Until she found another job, in another town.

Away from Cam.

She couldn't think about Cam. If she did she'd weaken. And she knew it was way past time for her to go. She rushed around the room, picking up the few personal items she'd left scattered around and stuffing them in the worn backpack.

"What are you doing?" Cam said from the doorway.

She stopped and looked at him. Stared at him for a moment, knowing that soon, she'd only see that face in her memory. "You know what I'm doing. I'm leaving."

"Delilah, I told you. The detective is gone and he won't be back. He has no reason to think you're here. That makes you as safe here as you are anywhere."

"That's not the only reason I'm leaving." She dropped her backpack and faced him. "I can't do this anymore, Cam. I thought I could but—I can't. I can't see you every day and know that you hate me. And that I deserve it."

He walked into the room and shut the door. "I don't hate you."

"I lied to you."

"I don't give a damn about that." He crossed the room to her. Stood in front of her, not touching her, but looking at her intently. Then he took her face in his hands. "The only thing I care about is this," he said, and kissed her.

His mouth moved over hers slowly, deliberately.

His tongue swept inside, taking possession, making her his. Sealing her to him, branding her soul. Her arms crept around his neck. She could no more resist him than she could stop breathing.

"Stay," he murmured, slipping his arms around her. "Stay with me."

She looked into his eyes, her heart in her throat. "I want to. More than I've ever wanted anything. But I can't." Oh, God. Her heart turned over in her chest. And broke.

"I love you, Delilah."

Her resistance crumbled into dust. She was lost, lost in his gaze, lost in the feel of his arms around her. In the sound of his voice saying he loved her.

His mouth crushed hers as he kissed her deeply, passionately. Her blood sizzled as she returned the kiss. One of his arms banded around her, holding her close, pressing her against him. His other hand closed over her breast and he kneaded it roughly. She couldn't think. Could hardly breathe. She only knew she wanted him. Needed him.

Loved him.

He backed her up against the wall. His leg slid between hers, his thigh felt hard and so good she nearly fainted. She rode his thigh as he kissed her, his tongue plunging deeply and retreating, mimicking lovemaking. She tightened her arms around his neck, holding on, never wanting to let go.

He let her slide down off his leg and she moaned and closed her eyes at the loss of contact. But then she felt him unzip her jeans, pull them down her legs. She kicked off her shoes and pulled the jeans the rest of the way off. He picked her up, his hands beneath her bottom, and she wrapped her legs around him, sex against sex. She could feel him thick and hard and straining beneath the denim.

They rocked together as they kissed, the friction between their bodies increasing until she couldn't wait any longer. He let her slide down again, then she fumbled with his pants, trying to get them undone. He had to push her hands aside and help her because his erection made it nearly impossible to get the jeans off. But he did.

He picked her up again, bracing them both against the wall, pulled the panties aside and slid home with a deep, hard thrust. The shock of him, the feel of him inside her almost undid her. She started convulsing immediately and he whispered things that only made her come harder as he stroked in and out of her. He bent his head and sucked on her nipple through her shirt and her bra, pulling hard until she thought her head was going to blow wide open.

He raised his head and their eyes locked. He pushed up and she drove herself down and she saw his eyes close and felt his muscles tighten and then he spasmed endlessly and filled her. Hot, hard, the tension built to another crest and she cried out his name as she came again.

THEY WERE LYING IN HIS BED, naked, and Cam knew he should get dressed and get back to work, but he didn't care. Martha and Gabe could handle the restaurant for a little longer. He wanted to make love to Delilah again. He looked at her and saw her watching him, her eyes solemn.

He rolled on his side, raising up on his elbow. Tracing a finger over her breast, lightly across her nipple, he watched it pearl. Her breasts were full and beautiful. He wondered what they'd be like if she were heavy with child. With his child. "We didn't use a condom. Could I have gotten you pregnant?"

"No. I had a shot." She smiled faintly at his puzzled look. "There's a birth control shot. It's good for several months."

He hadn't known. Why would he? He hadn't trusted a woman enough to take her word for it on what she used for birth control.

"I'm healthy," she said. "I had a blood test. So did

he. He insisted on it before we got ma—" She broke off, and her gaze fell.

"Delilah, look at me." He waited until she did to continue. "I meant it when I said I love you. I want you to marry me."

Her eyes searching his, she was quiet for a long moment. "If I file for divorce he'll find me. Maybe not immediately but eventually, he'll find me."

He couldn't deny it. "Yes. But then you'll be free."

He wanted to reassure her, promise to protect her, but he knew there was still a risk as well as she did. And ultimately, she had to reach the decision by herself.

Her gaze was solemn. Then she smiled, the sun breaking over the water. "I love you, Cam. I'll marry you."

After that there was nothing left to do but make love to her.

A LONG TIME LATER, Delilah got up and began to get dressed. "Can you leave Gabe and Martha in charge of the restaurant for a while longer?" she asked Cam.

He was still lying in bed, watching her. Wearing a sexy smile and nothing else. She couldn't help smiling back.

"Probably. Why?"

"I want you to take me to the police station. To talk to Maggie."

"Are you sure about that?"

"There's no reason not to, now that I've decided to file for divorce. He's going to know where I am soon enough. There's no reason not to go to the police now."

He got up and pulled on his jeans. "Are you going to press charges, then?"

"Yes. And I'm going to tell Maggie about his first wife. Even if they never prove it, at least I'll have tried." She sighed and picked up the backpack. "I got away from him. She never had a chance."

He zipped his jeans, then walked over and kissed her. "You're doing the right thing. The police can help you. Protect you. And so will I."

He had a lot more faith in the police than she did, but she let that go. It didn't matter. She'd made up her mind that loving Cam and being with him was worth any risk she had to take.

Half an hour later they were sitting in the station waiting for Maggie to get there. Ten minutes after that, she walked in looking very much at ease and in charge. She glanced at Cam, then turned that sharp cop's gaze on Delilah. She didn't look particularly happy to see her.

Big surprise.

Maggie nodded at both of them, then sat in her chair on the other side of the battered desk. "Sorry it took me so long. We had a cow in the middle of town and we couldn't locate the owner."

Cam smiled. "Mr. Eibert's?"

"Who else?" She smiled back at him and Delilah was struck by how much the smile changed her expression. She looked soft, feminine. And nothing like a cop.

No wonder she doesn't like me, Delilah thought. *She's in love with Cam.*

"What can I do for you? You didn't say what this was about when you called, Cam." Neither of them spoke. Maggie looked from one to the other. "Why don't we take this to an interview room," she said after a moment.

As soon as they were seated in the small room, bare except for a desk, chairs and a coffeemaker, Delilah began. She saw no reason to beat around the bush. "I want to file charges against my husband. For assault, or abuse, or whatever it's called."

To her credit, Maggie did no more than blink. "You have rights under the Texas family violence statutes. If a judge believes the charges have merit, then your husband can be arrested." She pulled out a form and started writing on it. "Are you in immediate danger?"

"She will be once he knows where she is," Cam said. "And she's afraid he'll figure that out once she files charges."

"Then you should ask for a restraining order. If there's a divorce pending—"

"There isn't. I went to a lawyer but I didn't file. My—he found out. That's when he—" She broke off, faltering under Maggie's steady gaze. "That's when he hurt me. As soon as I find a lawyer here, I'm going to file for divorce."

"I can take care of getting a temporary restraining order," Maggie said.

"Once that's issued he can't come near her?" Cam asked.

"That's right. If he violates it I can arrest him." She wrote something down and said, "But the temporary order is only good for two weeks. Once you file for divorce, your lawyer will ask for a permanent order of protection." She waited a minute and added, "Have you considered going to a shelter? I can give you a list of shelters in the area—"

"No. I won't go to one," Delilah said. "I had a friend in an abusive relationship. She went to a shelter. She's dead now. Her boyfriend found it, followed her to the bus stop and shot her."

Maggie was quiet for a moment, then she said, "I'm sorry. But regardless of what happened to your friend, that's the exception rather than the rule."

"He'll find me whether I go to a shelter or not. That's one reason I haven't been to the police. Because I didn't want him to find me." But in order to get on with her life, she had to face the fact that in all likelihood he'd discover where she was. And would come after her. Though she was determined to see it through, the thought of facing Avery again made her stomach tighten with nerves.

"I can only assure you that we'll do our best to enforce the order of protection and ensure your safety."

She said it stiffly and Delilah knew she'd offended her.

"That wasn't a slam against your department, Maggie," Cam said. "Once you hear Delilah's story you'll know why she's so scared of the bastard."

"I'm a cop, Cam. I'm familiar with the dangers of family violence." She opened a drawer and pulled out a notebook. Picked up a pen and said, "All right. Tell me what happened."

Delilah hadn't expected it to be easy to tell her story again, and especially not to someone already hostile to her. But she had to admire Maggie. Whatever she thought about Delilah, she took her statement without any indication that Delilah was anything other than a woman needing her professional help. And while it wasn't easy, Delilah did find some satisfaction in finally telling the story to the police.

Delilah didn't go into detail, she just told her what Avery had done, baldly and without embellishment. It didn't take long, especially since she didn't tell her about the murder. No, she'd save that for later.

When she finished, she looked at Maggie, waiting for the questions to begin.

"Did you go to the police?"

Delilah shook her head.

"A hospital?"

"No. I didn't go to anyone. I ran like hell because I was afraid I'd killed him. And if I hadn't, I knew he'd kill me. So I ran."

"If he died in the fall—"

"He didn't," Delilah interrupted. "Cam let me use his computer. I didn't find any mention of his death." She shuddered. "Besides, I know he's alive because he hired a private investigator to look for me. He came to the Scarlet Parrot."

"The P.I. said Freeman filed a missing person's report on Delilah," Cam said.

"That's why I wouldn't give you my license that day," Delilah told Maggie. "I was afraid he had."

Maggie didn't quite smile. "Under the circumstances, I don't think we'll let Mr. Freeman know we've found his missing wife." She made some more notes, then looked at Delilah. "Anything else?"

"Yes." She looked at Cam, then back to Maggie. "I think Avery killed his first wife."

CHAPTER NINETEEN

MAGGIE BLINKED. "Why didn't you tell me this to begin with?"

Delilah looked down at her hands, clasped together in her lap. "I was afraid you wouldn't believe me. And I have no proof, just suspicions."

"She may not have any proof," Cam put in, "but she has good reason to believe he killed the woman."

Maggie flicked him a glance. "I need to hear this from Delilah."

He gave Maggie a long look, but didn't say anything else.

"Why do you think he murdered his wife?"

"He said she died in a car accident, that she ran off the road when she was driving drunk. That was the excuse he gave me for getting rid of my car. That he was scared I'd have an accident like she did."

She reached down for her backpack, unzipped it and pulled out the diary. Laid it on Maggie's desk and said, "Her name was Anita. This is her diary. I found it when he locked me up."

Maggie didn't touch it. "Something in the diary leads you to believe he killed her?"

Delilah nodded. "She was allergic to alcohol in any form."

Maggie frowned. "That's all you have?"

"No. I know what he said to me when he found out I'd been to the lawyer. He said I wasn't going to divorce him. He said that that bitch Anita had thought she could divorce him but she'd found out different. He'd taught her respect before she died. And then he laughed and said I'd better be careful, that accidents happen all the time."

Maggie sighed and tapped her pen on the desk. "All right, it's suspicious. But it's a long way from proof. Do you know anything about this accident?"

"Just what I read in the papers on the Internet. It was ruled accidental death. Her car went off an embankment and exploded on impact." She went on to tell her what she'd told Cam. "It wasn't an accident," she finished. "It was cold-blooded murder."

Maggie stared at her for a long moment. Delilah couldn't tell what she was thinking. She looked, if anything, a little dense, but Delilah didn't think for one minute that Maggie Barnes was dumb.

Finally she sighed. "All right. I have a friend in the Houston PD, I'll see what she can find out."

Cam and Delilah exchanged glances. "There could be a problem with that," Cam said. "And with arresting him on the assault charges, too. Can you do that, or will the Houston police arrest him?"

"Houston."

"Damn. There's no way you can do it?"

Maggie shook her head. "I can ask for the warrant but Houston will serve it. What's the problem?"

"He has friends in the police department," Delilah said. "I don't know who they are, but I got the impression they were important."

"What are you suggesting? Are you saying the police had knowledge of his crime and covered it up?"

For the first time, Maggie showed some emotion and that emotion was anger. Well, she was a cop, what had Delilah expected?

"No." Not necessarily, she thought, but it was possible. "I'm saying he has friends and if there's an inquiry into the accident, he might find out. For all I know, they could warn him that there's a warrant out for his arrest."

"First murder, now police corruption," Maggie muttered. "What the hell do you expect me to do if you tie my hands like this? Call the Rangers in to investigate the department? On your say-so?"

"I didn't say they did anything wrong. And I don't care about that. All I care about is that Avery is charged with assault and that someone tries to find out if he murdered his first wife."

"Then you're going to have to let me talk to my friend. I can't find out any more about that accident than anyone else. It's a closed accident case from over a year ago and it's not even in my county."

Delilah looked at Cam. "You've come this far," he said. "I think you have to trust Maggie."

"Maggie's not the one I don't trust."

"I went to cop school with this woman. I know her, she's a friend of mine. And if there's anything I'm sure of, it's that she's a good cop."

You've come this far, Cam had said. She had to trust, had to hope that it would work out for the best. "All right," she said reluctantly. "Talk to her."

Maggie nodded briskly. "Don't expect any quick results on that."

"What about the other charges? What are the chances that he'll be prosecuted?"

"That's not my department. You need a lawyer."

"Come on, Maggie," Cam said. "You're bound to have an idea."

She hesitated, looked from one to the other. "You won't like it," she told them both. "With no proof, no witnesses, no photos, no doctor or hospital visits, and especially given the fact he's likely to have a slick lawyer, chances are the charges will be dropped."

Delilah felt sick. Why hadn't she at least taken pictures? But she'd been so scared, so sick, so worn out just surviving, she hadn't thought of it.

"I'm a witness," Cam said harshly. "I saw his goddamn fingerprints on her neck."

"That will help. The fact that Delilah is living with you and involved with you won't."

"Damn it, Maggie—" Cam said hotly.

She held up a hand. "Calm down. You asked and I told you what I know. What I've seen happen. I can't help that it's not what either of you wanted to hear."

She looked at Delilah and her tone gentled. "Get a good lawyer. That's the best thing you can do. That and go to a shelter." She gave Delilah a legal pad. "Write down anything you can think of, anything we didn't cover, that you think might be pertinent to either charge. I'll let you know when the warrant will be served." She hesitated and added, "What happens depends on the judge. If he believes your story, then the charges will stick."

"I have to hope he will, then," Delilah said, determined not to think about what would happen if he didn't.

Maggie got up and spoke to Cam. "Cam, could I see you for a minute? In the other room?"

"Took the words out of my mouth. I won't be long," he told Delilah and leaned down to kiss her. "Don't worry," he said quietly. "Everything's going to be okay."

But he looked grim as he followed Maggie out of the interview room.

"WHAT THE HELL is the matter with you?" Cam asked Maggie as soon as they were out of Delilah's earshot.

Maggie didn't answer. She took him into another room and closed the door. "Sit down," she said mildly. "We need to talk."

"Thanks, I'll stand. I don't intend to be here that long. Why did you do that? Why did you let her believe she did it for nothing?"

"Because sometimes that's what happens. She needs to be aware of that, especially since charging him will probably send the man into a tailspin. The most dangerous time for an abused woman is when she leaves her abuser."

"She knows that. Why the hell do you think she went into hiding?"

"Did you want me to lie to her?"

"I don't know." He took a frustrated turn. "This is bullshit."

"This is the system. Nobody ever said it was perfect."

Cam said something brief and crude.

Maggie let him fume a minute, then spoke. "Have you thought about what you're doing? Really thought about it?"

He turned to look at her. "What do you mean?"

"You're stepping into a situation that could be a disaster. At best you're going to be at the center of what promises to be a very nasty divorce. At worst it could mean Delilah's life. Or yours."

Incredulous, he stared at her. "What do you expect me to do? Abandon her? I'm in love with her."

"Believe me, that's clear as crystal."

"There's no way I'm letting her face all this alone. I can't believe you'd think I would."

Up to now she'd been glaring at him but now her expression softened. "I know you wouldn't." She put her hand on his arm and squeezed. "And I'm not saying you should. But the whole thing is a nightmare, Cam. It has the potential to be very dangerous for both of you."

"I can protect myself. And Delilah."

"Don't blow me off, Cam. Be careful. Try to convince her to go to a shelter."

"You heard her. That's not happening. Besides, that's a stopgap solution at best. She can't live in a shelter the rest of her life."

"No, she can't. But she might until we find out if Avery Freeman will be charged with the murder of his wife."

"What do you think the chances are that he will?"

"I have no way of knowing that until I talk to my friend and she does a little research on the matter."

"Do you think he did it?"

"I don't know that either. I can see that you and Delilah believe it. But since all I know about the case is what Delilah told me, I can't say."

"You'll let us know as soon as you hear anything?"

"Of course I will. In the meantime, get her a lawyer. A good one."

"I will."

Maggie nodded. As he walked to the door she spoke his name.

"Cam?"

He stopped and turned around.

"Does she make you happy?"

He smiled. "Yeah. She does."

"Good. You deserve it."

He smiled again and went out.

"MAGGIE DOESN'T BELIEVE ME about the murder, does she?" Delilah asked Cam once they were on their way back to the restaurant.

He shot her a glance, then looked back at the road. "I don't know. She said she had no way of knowing until she talks to her friend in Houston."

"She surprised me today," Delilah admitted. "I didn't expect her to be so…understanding."

"Maggie's a good person. And a good cop."

"I didn't think she'd be that nice. Especially considering she's in love with you."

He stopped at a stop sign and looked at her. "No, she's not. We've been through this before. She cares about me, sure. But she's not in love with me."

Delilah didn't believe that but she let it ride. "She thinks you're crazy to get involved with me, doesn't she?"

He sighed. "Delilah, quit worrying. What Maggie thinks or doesn't think doesn't matter. What matters is that we love each other and we're going to be together."

"I feel guilty." There, she'd finally said it. What had been bothering her since they'd gone to the station. "I should never have involved you. What if Avery comes after me? What if he hurts you when he's trying to get to me?"

He pulled into the carport and turned off the

truck. "Honey, I can take care of myself. You don't need to worry about that."

"But I do. I couldn't bear it if he hurt you. If something happened to you because of me."

"Nothing's going to happen to either of us."

They got out. "Cam, wait." He came around to where she stood by the truck.

"This is nerves, Delilah." He clasped her hands between his and brought them to his lips. "And God knows, you're entitled. You just finished talking about the worst time of your life. But it's over. You're safe now."

"I should go to a shelter."

"I thought you didn't want to do that."

"I don't. But if I go, that means you'll be safe."

He sighed and slipped his arms around her. She put her head against his chest, her arms around his waist, and closed her eyes. For a long moment they just held each other.

"Maggie thinks you should go. At least until we find out if he'll be facing murder charges on top of the family violence. She made me promise to try to talk you into it."

"I'll go." She pulled back enough to look at him. "Tomorrow. After Maggie tells us they've issued the family violence warrant." Avery was unlikely to find her before that. But once he was arrested and made bail…then he'd track her down. And she didn't want to be anywhere near Cam when he found her.

Cam kissed her. "We'll take tonight. And once this is over, we'll have all the tomorrows."

CHAPTER TWENTY

THE NEXT MORNING, Cam got up early and called Maggie to get the contact number of the shelter. After that, he called Gabe and asked him to come stay with Delilah while he ran an errand. Cam had brought him up to date after he and Delilah had gotten back from the station.

"I don't expect anything to happen yet," Cam told his brother when he came over. "But I didn't want to leave Delilah alone. She went through the wringer yesterday and she's still pretty shaky."

"No problem."

"There's fresh coffee," he said, waving a hand at the coffeepot. "Delilah's still asleep and I don't want to wake her, so when she gets up tell her I left some numbers for her by the phone in here. I think the lawyer will see her today, given the circumstances."

"Still kind of hard to believe," Gabe said. "The guy must be seriously wacko."

"Yeah." He frowned and rubbed his jaw. "Whether they can prove it or not is another matter."

"You okay with her going to a shelter?"

"I'm not happy about not seeing her, but I want her to be safe. Maggie thinks that's the safest place for her."

"Why can't you see her?"

"They don't much like for men to hang around those shelters. But I might be able to work something out. Anyway, if he's charged with murder, she won't be there long."

"And if he's not?"

"I guess we'll cross that bridge when we come to it." And hope like hell they didn't have to. "Whatever happens, I'm going to marry her the minute she's free of that bastard."

Gabe smiled. "Now there's a shock."

"You okay with that?" He was sure Gabe had gotten over his problems with Delilah, but he still wanted to hear it from him.

He put out his hand. "Since you're so gone on her, I guess I'd better be."

"Good." He grinned as they shook. "Because you're going to be my best man."

"CAMERON, WHAT ARE YOU DOING out so early?" Meredith Randolph said when she opened her kitchen door.

"I came to see how you were," he told her, kissing her on the cheek before walking in. "No more indigestion?"

"No, thank God. But you know that, since I talked to you the day before yesterday. Why are you really here?"

"Can't a guy come see his mother? And I'd take a cup of that coffee."

She poured him a mug and he took it to sit at the table. He looked at her more carefully than usual. Something was different about her, but he couldn't put his finger on it. "You look awfully pretty this morning."

She wore a light blue robe that complimented her fair coloring. A few years ago she'd decided to go blond and the switch had taken years off her age.

She laughed. "Thank you. Now I'm really curious about what you want."

"We'll get to that."

"Before we do there's something I should tell—"

A man about his mother's age or a little older walked into the kitchen, buttoning his shirt. "Meredith, what do you say we fly up to Dallas for the evening and—"

He stopped talking when he caught sight of Cameron. "Hello. You must be one of Meredith's sons." He shot her a quick glance and smiled. "You look just like her."

Cam stood up and offered a hand, though he was still in shock. Although the man was dressed, mostly, his mother still wore her robe and he didn't need to see the blush stealing into her cheeks to know the guy had spent the night.

"Cameron Randolph. But you have the advantage of me. I don't have a clue who you are."

"Cameron!"

The man grinned as they shook hands. "John Boyd. Good to meet you."

"Really, Cameron, that was rude." She got up as well and walked over to her guest.

"Now, now, Meredith," Boyd said before Cam could speak. "There's nothing wrong with a son looking out for his mother. I wouldn't give you two cents for one who didn't."

"I don't care, he doesn't need to be rude about it. I didn't raise ill-mannered children," she said with a glare for Cam. "John is my neighbor," she added.

Boyd laughed. "Better come clean, my dear. Your son looks like he wants to skewer me."

"Come clean?" Cam asked, still stunned. He knew his mother dated occasionally, but he'd never been face to face before with the obvious evidence that she had a lover. He wished he wasn't now.

Boyd took Cam's mother's hand and drew it

through his arm, patting it. He beamed down at her fondly. "I've asked your mother to marry me. She hasn't given me her answer yet, but I hope she will soon."

Cameron blinked, having a hard time taking everything in. His mother, married again? She'd been a widow for years. He couldn't imagine her married to another man besides his father. She'd always said he was the love of her life and she doubted she'd ever find a man to match him.

"Isn't this kind of sudden? No offense, but none of her family has even heard of you." He turned to his mother. "Have they?"

"There hasn't really been time," Meredith said. "John only moved in a few weeks ago."

"You're planning to marry a man you've only known a matter of weeks?" He was going to marry a woman he'd only known a short time, but that was different. This was his mother they were talking about.

She lifted her chin. "I'm considering it, yes. And I don't need to remind you I'm perfectly capable of making my own decisions."

Boyd looked from one to the other. "I think I'll leave you two alone to talk things over." Cam watched critically as he kissed her. "Call me later and we'll decide about going to Dallas. I have tickets to the symphony. Nice to meet you, Cameron."

"How do you know this guy isn't after your money?" Cam asked her bluntly once he left. His father had left his mother very well-off, and Cam had more than once worried about people, especially men, taking advantage of her.

Meredith laughed. "Oh, you should see your face. Honey, he has far more money than I do. You don't have to worry about that."

"Are you sure? How do you know this man's not scamming you?"

"Positive. John made his fortune in shipping. If you paid any attention to the papers you'd know the name."

"I pay attention," he said. Come to think of it, he did recognize the name. The guy was a multimillionaire, at least. "Are you sure he's who he claims to be?"

"You heard him talk about flying to Dallas?"

Cam nodded.

"He wants to go in his private jet. I've been in it before, Cameron. He's the real thing."

Okay, the guy was loaded. That still didn't mean Cam approved of him. "Has anybody else met him?"

"You mean your brother and sisters? Yes. Cat met him and liked him very much. Neither Gabe nor Gail has met him yet, but they will soon. And no one but you knows he's asked me to marry him. I'd appreciate it if you didn't tell them, either. I intend to do that myself."

"Fine by me, I don't want to be the one to spill this news." Although he wouldn't mind being around to see their reactions. "But Mom, this isn't like you. I mean, you hardly know this guy."

"I feel as if I've known him all my life." She sighed and looked what he could only describe as starry-eyed. It boggled his mind.

"I'm having so much fun. He's mad about me," she said with a satisfied smile. "I fell in love with him at first sight." She looked at Cam a bit defensively. "I suppose you think that's crazy."

Cam suddenly realized what was different about her. She looked happier than she had since his father had died, so many years ago.

"Actually, I don't think it's crazy at all."

"You don't?" She looked surprised.

"No." He hugged her. "If you love him, you should go for it." He waited a moment and added, "As long as you're sure he's not after your money."

She laughed and patted his cheek. "I'd have married him anyway, but it's nice to know you won't be angry. I hope Gabe takes the news as well as you did."

Cam grinned. "Should be interesting."

"Let's go in the den and sit down and you can tell

me why you came over. I know there's more to it than just a surprise visit."

Once in the den he didn't sit down, he was too restless. Instead, he walked over to the windows and glanced out at the ocean before looking back to his mother. "Do you still have Grandmother's ring?"

"Livia's engagement ring?" she asked, referring to his father's mother. "Of course I do. What—" She stopped and stared at him, her eyes round with shock. "Cameron, are you getting married?"

He smiled. "Yeah." He might not know when, but he knew it was going to happen.

"It's Delilah, isn't it?"

"Of course it's Delilah. Who else have I been living with the past few weeks?"

"You haven't known her any longer than I've known John. Are you sure you know what you're doing?"

"I'm sure I love her. And that she loves me."

Her eyes sparkled and he knew she was about to cry.

"I'm so glad. I was afraid you were never going to get married." She pulled a tissue from her pocket and dabbed at her eyes. "You didn't ask for your grandmother's ring when you asked Janine to marry you."

"No, I didn't." Janine had wanted a ring of her

own. Actually, she'd wanted a rock he couldn't really afford. Which should have warned him. "My subconscious must have known what it was doing."

"I never liked her, you know."

"Janine? You never let on."

Meredith shrugged. "It wasn't my business to tell you. You were a grown man, after all. But I never thought she was right for you."

"You could have said something."

"Would you have listened?"

He thought about that. He'd been convinced he really wanted to marry Janine. "Probably not."

"No, you wouldn't have. And then you'd have been mad at me for interfering."

Which was true, but he didn't want to talk about Janine anymore. "Forget Janine. She's not important now."

"No, Delilah's the important one now." She went over to him and hugged him. "When are you planning to ask her?"

"I already did. But I can't give her the ring yet. There's a problem."

"A big one?"

"Yeah. A big one," he said, and told her.

When he finished, his mother stared at him so long he thought she was in shock. Finally she said, "I can hardly believe it. That poor girl. When I think about what she endured at that monster's hands—" She broke off, shuddering. "It's a miracle she was able to escape."

Cam nodded grimly. "I just hope they're able to get proof he killed his first wife." That would be far and away the best thing for Delilah. So he'd be locked up and never able to hurt her again. "I need to get back home. Hopefully Delilah will have reached the lawyer and she can see him today."

"I'll go get your grandmother's ring. This would make her very happy."

"Thanks. And Mom?" She looked at him over her shoulder. "Tell John if he doesn't treat you right Gabe and I will kick his ass."

She laughed. "I'll warn him. But you don't have to worry. He's a wonderful man."

DELILAH WOKE UP SLOWLY and stretched. Opened her eyes to a single pale pink rose on the pillow beside her. She sat up and held it to her nose, smiling. She couldn't imagine where Cam had gotten it at that time of the morning. Unless he'd raided someone's garden. The gesture was so sweet it brought tears to her eyes.

Then she remembered she had to leave him and that nearly did her in. But she had decided the night before that she wasn't going to have a defeatist attitude. She would believe that Avery would be arrested. He would be charged with murder and then she and Cam could start their lives together.

A few minutes later she stumbled into the kitchen in search of coffee. She halted on the threshold. Instead of Cam, Gabe sat at the table, reading the paper and drinking a cup of coffee.

He doesn't hate you anymore, she reminded herself. Probably. Cam didn't think so, anyway. But she still didn't feel quite comfortable around him.

"Hi," she said cautiously on her way to the coffeemaker. "Where's Cam?"

"I don't know. Said he had to run an errand and asked me to come stay with you."

"I don't need babysitting."

He flashed her a grin and she thought he was pretty cute when he wasn't being a jerk.

"Tell that to Cam."

She took her coffee and sat at the table. "I'm sorry he got you over here. I'm sure you have better things to do than babysit me."

"I don't mind." She lifted an eyebrow. "I figure I owe you."

"Why?

"I was kind of hard on you. Before…well, before."

She smiled at his phrasing. "You were looking out for Cam. I don't blame you for that." She waited a moment, then added, "Besides, you were right. I lied to him."

"You made a mistake. Happens to everybody." He folded the paper and laid it on the table. "It wasn't you exactly. I used to know a woman..." He shrugged. "You reminded me of her."

"Who was she?"

He smiled wryly. "You know those mistakes we just talked about? I've made a lot of them. She was the worst."

Delilah started to say something but someone knocked on the back door.

"I'll get it," Gabe said.

"Hey, Maggie," she heard him say as he let her in.

"Hey, Gabe. Delilah."

"Want some coffee?" Gabe asked her.

"Thanks." While Gabe got a coffee cup down and filled it, she spoke to Delilah. "The warrant has been issued for Avery Freeman's arrest for violating the family violence laws. I should be hearing that they picked him up before long."

At least that was something. "What about the other?" Delilah asked hopefully. "Have you found out anything about the murder?"

Accepting the cup from Gabe, Maggie shook her head. "No, nothing. It might take my friend a while to check into it. Plus, she can't ask for help since she isn't sure of Freeman's contacts. Added to that, she's doing everything on the q.t. I don't think it's going to be a fast process."

Delilah tried for a smile but wasn't very successful. "Too much to hope for."

"Did Cam give you the number of that shelter?"

"I haven't seen him this morning."

"He left it by the phone," Gabe said. "Along with the lawyer's number. He said you should try to make the appointment for today."

"All right. I'll call him right now."

Maggie started to say something but static from her two-way radio cut in. "Barnes," she answered.

A disembodied, nasal voice said, "Ten-fifty-four in progress at Main and Redbird. Do you copy?"

She rolled her eyes. "Ten-four. Have someone else take it. I'm tied up right now."

"Negative. Officer Barnes, you're to proceed immediately to the location."

"It's a damn cow in the road," Maggie said. "The same cow that's been in the road every day this week. What's the rush? It's not an emergency."

"Since no one else was around the chief had to go over there to handle it," the dispatcher said with a distinct tremor in her voice. "The cow did its business on his foot. Then it stepped on the other foot. He's not happy."

Maggie winced. "Ten-four. Over and out." She looked at Delilah. "Great. He's going to be in one hell of a mood. I better go. I'll let you know as soon as I'm notified they have Freeman in custody."

"Thank you." When Maggie left, Delilah went to the phone and picked up the paper Cam had left her. "I'm going to make those calls and then shower."

"Okay. Anything need doing down in the restaurant?"

"The tea maker wasn't working very well last night. It kept spitting every time you'd fill a glass. Think you could fix it?"

"Depends. I can try. Sometimes I think that thing's possessed."

Half an hour later she went downstairs. As she walked through the kitchen and toward the doorway to the main room, she heard the murmur of voices. Thinking Cam must have returned, she started to go in but Gabe's raised voice stopped her.

"Sorry, we don't open until eleven."

"That's unfortunate," a man said.

Delilah's heart began to pound. She clung to the doorjamb and strained to hear more. It couldn't be him. She was imagining things.

"Hey, I said we were clo—" Gabe broke off with a queer groan.

Delilah didn't wait. She dashed across the kitchen and grabbed the phone, punching in numbers with trembling hands. Let me be wrong, she prayed. Don't let it be Avery. Let me feel like a fool for calling 9-1-1 for nothing.

"I wouldn't," he said from the doorway. "Not unless you'd like me to finish off your friend. I believe he's alive but that can easily change."

She turned around slowly, holding the phone against her chest. Tall, good-looking. Mid-forties with a glint of silver in his carefully cut brown hair. He looked like exactly what he was. A successful, powerful man.

A murderer.

"Hello, Anne," Avery Freeman said, the gun in his hand pointing at her heart. "Surprised to see me, darling?"

CHAPTER TWENTY-ONE

DELILAH STOOD frozen.

"Hang up the phone, Anne," Avery said, gesturing at her with his free hand. "Do it or he's a dead man."

She finally found her voice. "What did you do to him, you bastard?"

"The phone, darling. Really, I must insist."

She hung up.

"Wise choice," Avery said approvingly. "We've discussed obedience before. There's something else we should have discussed. Come, into the other room so I can keep an eye on your friend as well."

She did as he said, feeling as if she were moving in quicksand. Gabe lay crumpled on the floor beside the bar, unmoving. She couldn't tell if he was alive. "You bastard," she said.

"You're repeating yourself. Who is he? Another man you've been whoring with?"

"I haven't—" She faltered at his snarl of rage.

He backhanded her across the mouth with his left hand. "Not only a whore but a lying whore."

Pain exploded, radiating up her cheek. Tears stung her eyes and she tasted blood. She watched Avery pull something from his coat pocket and toss it on the bar.

"Look at them. Pictures of you and another man," he said, his voice thick with barely contained rage. "The man who owns this place. Cameron Randolph. You let him put his hands on you. Let him kiss you. Let him f—"

"Stop it!"

He kept going, his words a hail of malice. "You betrayed me. Betrayed your marriage vows. I could kill you for that."

"I betrayed nothing. What we have isn't a marriage. It's a mockery. Of everything decent."

He laughed. "You're one to talk about decency, my dear, cheating wife."

Gabe groaned, drawing Avery's attention. He shoved at him with his foot. "Waking up, are you?"

Gabe's eyes flickered open. A moment later Delilah saw awareness dawn. "Leave him alone. He works here. He's nothing to me. You don't have any reason to hurt him."

"I hate to point this out, my darling Anne, but I can't trust your word. How do I know you haven't slept with him as well?"

"I haven't. I swear I haven't."

"What about this one?" He gestured at the pictures. "Are you saying you didn't have sex with Cameron Randolph? Think carefully before you deny it." He swung the gun toward Gabe. Smiled at her and said, "Lie to me and he dies."

Delilah met Gabe's gaze. He shook his head, as if to say, don't do it. But she had no choice. She couldn't let Gabe die because of her. Not if she could possibly stop it. And Cam… She prayed harder than she'd ever prayed that he wouldn't walk in that door.

"Yes. I did."

"Say it. Say it!" he snarled.

"I slept with another man."

He slapped her again, even harder than the first time. She staggered, stifled a cry. A cruel smile stretched his mouth. "Before I'm finished with you, you'll wish you'd never been born. I hope he was worth it."

"He was." She raised her head and looked him in the eye. If she was going to die, she wouldn't do it sniveling. "I'm divorcing you, Avery. I filed charges against you. The police know you're here. They're on their way," she lied.

He shook his head. "A pitiful attempt. Well, we won't be here long. Just long enough to kill your lover. I'll enjoy watching you when I do. I'll think of something particularly painful for your…entertainment. Then we'll go to Mexico. I hear there are some very remote places. No one to hear you scream. Except me, of course."

She blocked his words, knowing if she thought about them she'd be paralyzed with fear. "The police know about Anita. I told them you killed her."

That shook his calm, but only for an instant. "No one will believe that. You're nothing. Less than nothing. A liar and a whore. Why would they believe you over me?"

She cast a sharp glance at Gabe, saw him watching Avery, waiting to make a move. He must know as well as she did that he wouldn't get more than one chance. "I found her diary and I gave it to the police. She was allergic to alcohol. She wasn't driving drunk. I know it," she said softly. "You know it. And now the police know it, too."

"Delilah, what's going—" Rachel came through the front door of the restaurant, halting when she saw the scene before her.

"Rachel, get out!" Delilah shouted, as Avery swung the gun toward the girl.

Rachel stood frozen, her mouth open and gaping in shock. Avery fired at her, but Gabe rushed him and spoiled his aim. The shot went wide, shattering the glass in the door. And the two men were locked in a desperate struggle for the gun.

"Call the police," Delilah shouted to Rachel. "Get out of here!"

Delilah didn't think she was going. She stood stock-still, her eyes wide open and terrified, and then long seconds later, she turned and fled.

Delilah pulled the bat from beneath the bar, with some wild idea of hitting Avery with it and somehow saving Gabe. But even as she ran toward them, the gun went off and Gabe fell back, a hand to his side. Avery brought the gun crashing down on his head. Gabe slumped to the floor just as she reached them.

She swung the bat at him but Avery jumped back. He pointed the gun at her. Panting, bleeding, he snarled, "Drop the bat or I'll kill you."

She laughed and held on to it. "Go ahead and try. You don't want me dead. Not yet."

His smile was pure malevolence. "That's true." He swung the weapon to point it at Gabe's back. "I want you alive. But I can kill him."

Gabe lay unmoving. Dying… Because of her. If Cam had been here, it would be him, dying on the floor of his restaurant. It still could be. He could walk in, unaware, at any moment. She could be the cause of his death, as well as his brother's.

"Don't kill him." She dropped the bat. It clattered onto the floor and rolled away.

His smile widened. "How do you plan to stop me, darling Anne?"

Her stomach pitched but she answered steadily. "If you let him live, I'll go with you willingly. I'll leave the country with you. I won't fight you."

"And if I kill him?"

Shrugging, she bargained for a man's life with the only thing she had. Her own life. "You'll have to kill me, too. Now. And lose out on your fun."

CAM TURNED INTO the parking lot of the Scarlet Parrot. He looked in the rearview mirror and saw Maggie's police car drive up behind him. He felt a tingle of unease crawl up his spine, but dismissed it. She had to be coming to tell them Freeman was in police custody. And about damn time, too. He parked the truck, then got out and went to meet her by the outside stairs to the restaurant.

When he saw her face, he knew something was wrong. "What happened, Maggie?"

"Freeman's missing," she said without preamble. "He disappeared before the Houston police could take him into custody."

He stared at her blankly for a minute, trying to take it in. "He's gone? When?"

"They don't know." She looked away, then back at him. He started up the stairs but Maggie grabbed his arm to stop him. "Cam, wait. We need—"

A sharp crack split the air, the sound of a car backfiring, but they both knew it was no car. It was a gunshot and it had come from inside the restaurant upstairs.

"Goddamn it!" He looked at Maggie. "That's him. He's got Delilah. And Gabe." Cam had his foot on the stairs when Rachel came tumbling down. She saw the two of them at the bottom and flung herself sobbing into Cam's arms.

"What happened?"

"She—he—oh, God. Oh, God, oh, God."

She was totally hysterical, almost gibbering. He shook her, hard, and she stopped and hiccuped, her eyes gazing into his, dilated with horror.

"Tell me. Calm down and tell me what you saw. Right now, Rachel."

"A man. He's got a gun." She sucked in more air. "I think—oh, God, I think he shot Gabe. He tried to shoot me but Gabe grabbed him."

"Where's Delilah?" he asked harshly. "Did he shoot her, too?"

"I don't know," Rachel wailed, putting her face in her hands. "I don't think so. She yelled at me to get out. But Gabe was bleeding and fighting him."

"The bastard has both of them," he said to Maggie, putting Rachel aside. She collapsed on the pavement, sobbing hysterically again.

Maggie wasn't listening. She had already pulled her two-way radio out of her pocket and was urgently requesting backup and medical assistance. She signed off and pulled her gun out of the holster. "You should call the clinic in case the EMTs don't get here. Ask one of the doctors to come."

"Rachel can do it. I'm going with you," Cam said.

She checked her weapon and gave him a furious glance. "The hell you are. You stay right here and call for help. I'm a cop. I'm trained for this and you're not."

"I don't give a shit who's trained and who's not. If you think I'm going to stand here and do nothing while that maniac is holding Delilah and Gabe at gunpoint, you're even crazier than he is."

"I'm not going to argue this with you. You could get killed."

"So could they." If they weren't already dead. He looked up the stairs, then back at Maggie. "We're wasting time. I'll go in the back way, up through the restaurant kitchen and draw his attention. You come through the front."

"You're a civilian. I could lose my job for letting you do this."

"Better your job than their lives."

She hesitated for a moment.

"Maggie, I'm going. Accept it."

She swore, then nodded. "All right. Stay out of my line of fire."

"If he's killed them—" Cam began.

"Don't think about it," she interrupted. "Fear makes you freeze. Just go up there and get his attention. I'll do the rest."

"If he's killed either of them he's a dead man, Maggie." He didn't wait for a response. He was going to save his brother and the woman he loved or die trying.

"YOU WON'T GET AWAY WITH IT, you know," Delilah told him. "Even if the police weren't already on their way they will be now. They'll be here before you can get away."

Keep talking, she thought. Babble, it doesn't matter. The longer she kept him talking, the better her chances. If she left the restaurant with him, she might as well sign her own death warrant.

"You think so? I haven't heard any sirens." He smiled widely, still pointing the gun at Gabe. "Besides, I'll have a hostage. Don't forget, you offered to go with me. They'll have to let me go."

"Don't count on it," Cam said from the kitchen doorway.

Both of them turned at the sound of his voice. Avery jerked up the gun, pointing it at him, but before he could shoot, Cam was on him. It was a horrifying replay of the scene minutes before when Gabe had been shot. Delilah watched the struggle with a hideous sense of déjà vu.

"Freeze! Police!" Maggie stood at the front door, arms outstretched, the gun in her hands pointed unwaveringly at the two men. They ignored her, each still struggling desperately for control of the gun.

"Delilah, get down," Maggie shouted and advanced toward them.

Delilah dropped to the floor. She heard another shot and saw Cam stagger back. *Oh, God, please don't let him be hurt,* she prayed. *Not Cam. Bad enough that Gabe could be dying.*

"Police! Drop it!" Maggie commanded.

Avery turned the gun on her. In slow motion, Delilah heard the crack of an explosion, saw blood blossom on his chest. He stood for a moment, the gun slack in his hand, bleeding, an expression of surprise on his face. The gun fell. He pitched forward and face-planted on the floor.

Seconds later she was in Cam's arms, sobbing,

clutching him, unable to believe he was there and he was safe.

"It's over. You're okay." He kissed her, repeated the words. "You're okay."

Tears were falling so fast she could hardly see him. "Gabe. I think he killed Gabe."

Cam left her to go to his brother. Delilah looked at her hands, realizing there was blood on them. Cam's blood. "Cam, you're bleeding."

"It's just my arm. It's nothing."

She got up shakily and walked over to them. Cam turned Gabe over and put his fingers on his neck. "He's got a pulse. His eyelids are fluttering. He's coming around." He looked at her. "Hand me something to staunch this blood. He's bleeding like stink."

Gabe groaned. "Not dead," she heard him say.

She grabbed the handiest thing, yanking a cloth from one of the tables, and gave it to Cam. She crouched down beside Gabe. "You idiot," she said. "Why did you do that? You could have been killed."

His grin was weak but still cocky. "You're welcome." He sat up, rubbing the back of his head and wincing. "Damn, Cam, what are you trying to do to me? My head is what's killing me. That's just a flesh wound." Looking down at the cloth Cam had packed on the wound, he added, "I think."

The sound of sirens filled the air. "Nice of them to show up," Cam said grimly. "After everything is over."

"Freeman's dead," Maggie said, kneeling beside the body. She got to her feet, pulled out her radio and spoke into it. "All clear. The gunman is dead. Request immediate medical assistance. At least one civilian is down." Pausing, she looked at Delilah. "Are you hurt? Did he shoot you?"

Delilah shook her head. "Gabe's hurt."

"One civilian down," she said, then signed off and came to help.

Cam was trying to make Gabe be still and let him put pressure on the wound, but Gabe wasn't cooperating.

Maggie pushed Cam aside. "Let me do this, Cam. I have some EMT training." When Cam didn't move she added, "See about your own wound. Delilah, put some pressure on that. And get some ice for your face after you do. Lie down and be still," she told Gabe.

"Maggie?" Delilah said. "If you hadn't been here, I don't know what we would have done. Thank you."

Her mouth tightened as she knelt beside Gabe. "I just wish I'd gotten here a little sooner. I came as soon as I heard he'd skipped town."

Cam took Delilah in his arms and kissed the top of her head. "I can't remember ever being that scared in my life. Thank God you're all right." He pulled back and looked at her, touched his fingers to her bruised cheek. "He'll never hurt you again."

"I can't believe it's over." She looked over at Avery's body and shuddered. Then she leaned back to meet Cam's eyes. "You could have been killed. Gabe almost was. It's my fault. I brought this on you. If I'd gone to a shelter in the first place—"

"Delilah, don't do this. If you do, he wins. Freeman's responsible for all of this, not you. He's the one who shot Gabe. Who shot me. He's the one who would have killed you." He kissed her mouth, very gently. "He's dead. It's over. And thank God that it is."

CHAPTER TWENTY-TWO

EVERYONE WENT to the hospital. Cam was treated and released, and though he'd insisted Delilah be examined, the doctor had said she was fine.

Gabe had been admitted and released the next day. The gunshot wound wasn't serious and had been treated immediately but the possible concussion from the blow to the head kept him there overnight.

It turned out Freeman had found Delilah not through his police contacts but through the private detective. Apparently the man had run into Rachel on his way out and had shown her Delilah's picture. Rachel had said Delilah worked there and then promptly forgot to mention it to either Cam or Delilah.

Several days after Freeman was killed, Delilah received a visit from his lawyer. He asked to see her alone, so Cam let them use his office. A short time later, the lawyer left and Delilah came out, looking shell-shocked.

"I inherited his entire estate. He died without a will, so it all comes to me."

He studied her. "You don't seem very pleased about it."

"I don't know what I am. I don't want his money. I was about to divorce him. It feels—" She gestured helplessly. "I don't know, wrong."

"Why, did he make it illegally?"

"No. No, it's legitimate. But…there's so much."

"Just out of curiosity, how much?"

"Three million dollars."

"Wow," he said when he found his voice.

"I don't know what I'm going to do about this," she said. "I have to think about it."

He wasn't sure what he thought about it either. His grandmother's engagement ring had been burning a hole in his pocket for days while he waited for the right time to ask Delilah to marry him. He'd finally settled on tonight.

Something told him she might be a little distracted. But he couldn't wait any longer. So he went ahead and made his plans. He conned Cat into making the two of them a romantic dinner, then surprised Delilah by having a late supper on the beach. The late-October night was mild, and the sand was dappled with moonlight from the full moon. It was a good choice. Quiet, deserted. Romantic.

They'd finished eating and she was sitting between his legs with his arms wrapped around her. From time to time, he picked up the wineglass beside them and fed her wine or took a sip himself.

"This is nice." She ran her fingers idly over his forearm and sighed. "How did you get Cat to make the dinner?"

"I told her I wanted to romance you. She's a sucker for that kind of thing."

Delilah laughed and kissed him. "Tell her it worked." They were quiet a while and then she said, "I think I've decided what to do about the money."

"What's that?" He didn't really want to talk about Freeman's money, but he resigned himself, knowing it would nag at her until she did.

"At first I was going to give it all away, but I decided that was a little melodramatic." He smiled and kissed the top of her head. "So I decided I'd do something good with it. Something that will help women like me. Like Anita."

"A shelter?"

"Maybe. I was thinking of a foundation that could do several things. Fund another shelter, or improve security in existing ones. And—"

She turned in his arms and looked at him and he could see excitement shining in her eyes. "A scholarship program. For battered women to attend college or graduate school. What do you think?"

"That sounds like a great idea. What are you going to call it?"

"Anita's fund," she said softly.

"I think she'd like that," he said, and kissed her.

"I'm not giving it all to the fund. I'm going to use some of it for me to go to school. I still want to be an accountant."

"So being independently wealthy hasn't changed your mind about that?"

She laughed. "Did you think it would?"

"I don't know. I wondered if you'd changed your mind about something else." He moved away from her so he could dig in his pocket. It took him a minute to locate the ring, but his fingers closed around it and he pulled it out.

He held it out to her. "About you and me."

She didn't take it. She stared at it, at him, and said, "That looks like an—" She cleared her throat and started again. "It's a ring."

He smiled. "That's right. My grandmother's engagement ring. Will you marry me, Delilah?"

She looked stunned. Could it really be such a huge surprise to her? The longer she stared at him in silent surprise the more nervous it made him.

"Delilah? Aren't you going to say something?"

Preferably yes. Or even, yes, Cam, I love you. Instead she just sat there, looking a little green around the gills.

"You're asking me to marry you."

"That's generally what a ring and a proposal mean. I asked you before, but I couldn't give you the ring." Why was she sitting there gazing at him as if he'd lost his ever-loving mind?

"I thought—when you didn't say anything I didn't know if you still wanted to."

"I want to marry you more than I've ever wanted anything else."

"Yes," she said. "Yes, I'll marry you." She wrapped her arms around his neck and kissed him.

"Thank God," he said, against her mouth. "You had me worried there for a minute."

She eased back and held out her hand. He slipped the ring on her finger. Kissed her knuckles, then turned her hand over and kissed her palm. "I love you, Delilah. I want to make you happy."

"You already have. I'm so happy I'm almost afraid to believe it's for real."

"Believe it."

She held out her hand and admired the ring, a simple diamond in an old-fashioned setting. "It's so beautiful. Did you say it was your grandmother's?"

He nodded. "I'm the eldest grandson, so she wanted it to come to me." Keeping her gaze, he added, "In case you're wondering, Janine never saw this ring."

Her smile grew even brighter. "I'm glad." She went into his arms and kissed him again.

Deepening the kiss, he slipped his tongue inside her mouth. Tasted her sweetness, rubbed his hand over her breasts. He wanted her now, soft, sweet, giving, surrendering to him in passion. In love.

They lay down and he kissed her again, slid his hand beneath her shirt to caress her breasts. "Have you ever made love on the beach?"

"No." Her hand slipped down to his fly and she stroked him. "Am I about to?" She stroked him again, harder this time.

"If you keep doing that you are." In about twenty seconds, in fact.

She smiled and did it again.

He rolled on top of her, settled between her thighs. "I want to see you wearing my ring." He kissed her, long and leisurely, feeling the heat build. "Only my ring."

A slow, wicked smile curved her mouth and she pulled his head down to hers. "I think I can manage that," she said, and kissed him.

A LITTLE OVER TWO WEEKS LATER, Delilah's wedding day dawned. She woke up slowly, in Cam's arms.

"Morning," he said, and kissed her. "Happy wedding day."

She smiled. "Happy wedding day to you, too. I still can't believe it's happening."

"Let me see if I can convince you," he said, rolling on top of her.

Someone pounded on the door before he could get started convincing. "That's probably Gabe," she said. "Coming to take you away."

"Tell me again why I have to leave?" he asked after he got dressed.

"Because your sisters said you had to," she told him, laughing.

"And if I didn't get you out of here, they'd nag me to death," Gabe added. "So let's go."

"I'll see you at the church," Cam told her and kissed her goodbye.

"Plenty of time for that later," Gabe said, dragging him away when he would have kissed her again.

After Gabe and Cam left, her soon-to-be sisters-in-law and mother-in-law arrived to help her get ready.

Cat, who was around her size, had offered to lend Delilah her wedding gown. When Delilah had protested, Cat had told her with a mischievous smile that the Randolphs were very traditional and she had to have something old, something new, something borrowed and something blue. The dress could be her something borrowed.

So Delilah accepted. The gown was beautiful and she was very touched Cat had wanted her to wear it.

Two hours after they had arrived, Delilah was nearly ready. The gown was deceptively simple, a strapless ivory satin with a sweetheart neckline and a long train of antique lace. Gail gave her a blue garter to wear for her something blue, and she wore Cam's grandmother's engagement ring as something old.

"But now you need something new," Gail said. "Mother's taken care of that."

Meredith handed her a long, narrow red velvet box.

Startled, Delilah looked at her. "Oh, I couldn't— It's so sweet of you, but—"

Meredith laughed. "It's tradition. You'll hurt my feelings if you don't accept it." Delilah still hesitated and Meredith added, "Your own mother couldn't be here, Delilah. Let me spoil you a little as I know she would have loved to do."

Delilah had to blink away tears before she opened the box. A delicate gold charm bracelet with a single charm dangling from it lay inside. "It's beautiful," she said, looking at the intricately designed charm. "It's a Chinese symbol, isn't it? I'm sorry, I don't know what it means." She looked at Meredith for enlightenment.

"It's the Chinese symbol for happiness." She smiled and fastened the bracelet around Delilah's wrist. "Cameron can add to it, but I wanted to start one for you. Gail and Cat will tell you I gave each of them one on their wedding days." She glanced at Gail.

"You didn't give it to me until my second wedding," Gail said. "When I married Jay."

"Yes, I know," Meredith said drily, and they all laughed.

"It's beautiful. Thank you," Delilah said, fighting tears.

"You've made my son very happy," Meredith said, and kissed her cheek. "And that makes me very happy, too."

"Now you've done it," Cat said, when Delilah started to cry. "She'll have to reapply her makeup."

"You've all been so sweet to me. You don't know what it means to me that Cam's family has been so kind."

"We love you, Delilah. You're part of our family now," Gail said.

"And the Randolphs stick together," Cat added, hugging her.

"Welcome to our family, Delilah," Meredith said.

An hour later, Delilah waited in the alcove at the Randolph family church in Aransas City, filled to overflowing. The wedding march started and she walked down the aisle to Cam's side, knowing she had everything she'd ever wanted, everything she'd ever imagined. Family, friends, and the man she loved waiting for her.

"You're more beautiful than I've ever seen you," Cam said when she reached his side.

"That's because I'm happier than I've ever been," she said, and put her hand in his.

* * * * *

Look for Gabe Randolph's story in
2006 wherever Harlequin books are sold.

HARLEQUIN *Super*ROMANCE®

COLD CASES: L.A.

A *new mystery/suspense miniseries* from

Linda Style,

author of The Witness
and The Man in the Photograph

His Case, Her Child
(Superromance #1281)

He's a by-the-book detective determined to find his
niece's missing child. She's a youth advocate equally
determined to protect the abandoned boy in her charge.
Together, Rico Santini and Macy Capshaw form an uneasy
alliance to investigate the child's past and, in the process,
unearth a black-market adoption ring at a shelter for
unwed mothers. The same shelter where years earlier
Macy had given birth to a stillborn son. At least,
that's what she was told....

Available in June 2005 wherever Harlequin books are sold.

HARLEQUIN®

AMERICAN *Romance*®

SARAH'S GUIDE TO LIFE, LOVE & GARDENING

by Connie Lane

(Harlequin American Romance #1072)

When Sarah Allcroft comes across an opportunity to be a gardener at Cupid's Hideaway, an Ohio bed-and-breakfast, she jumps at it. And when she meets the handsome local police chief, she realizes she might be able to brush up on more than her gardening.

Available in June 2005
wherever Harlequin books are sold.

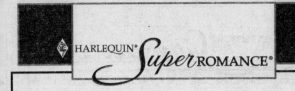

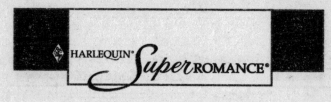

#1278 STRANGER IN TOWN • Brenda Novak
A Dundee, Idaho, book

Hannah Russell almost killed Gabe Holbrook in a car accident. Gabe's been in a wheelchair ever since, his athletic career ended. He's a recluse, living in a cabin some distance from Dundee, and Hannah can't get over her guilt. But one of her sons is on the high school football team and when Gabe—reluctantly—becomes the coach, she finds herself facing him again....

#1279 HIS REAL FATHER • Debra Salonen
Twins

Lisa never had trouble telling the Kelly brothers apart. Even though they were twins, they were nothing alike. Joe was quiet, and Patrick the life of the party. Each was important to her. But only one was the father of her son.

#1280 A FAMILY FOR DANIEL • Anna DeStefano
You, Me & the Kids

Josh White is trying to care for his late sister's son, but Daniel's hurting so much nothing seems to reach him. The only person the boy responds to is Amy Loar, Josh's childhood friend. Amy has her own problems, but she does her best to help. Then Daniel's father shows up and threatens to sue for custody, and the two old friends have to figure out how to make a family for Daniel.

#1281 HIS CASE, HER CHILD • Linda Style
Cold Cases: L.A.

He's a by-the-book detective determined to find his niece's missing child. She's a youth advocate equally determined to protect an abandoned boy in her charge. Together, Rico Santini and Macy Capshaw form an uneasy alliance to investigate the child's past, and in the process they unearth a black-market adoption ring at a shelter for unwed mothers. The same shelter where years earlier Macy had given birth to a stillborn son. At least, that's what she was told....

#1282 THE DAUGHTER'S RETURN • Rebecca Winters
Lost & Found

Maggie McFarland's little sister was kidnapped twenty-six years ago, but Maggie has never given up hope of finding Kathryn. Now Jake Halsey has a new lead for her, and it looks as if she's finally closing in on the truth. The trouble is, it doesn't look as if Jake has told her the truth about *himself*.

#1283 PREGNANT PROTECTOR • Anne Marie Duquette
9 Months Later

The stick said positive. She was pregnant. Lara Nelson couldn't believe it. How had she, a normally levelheaded cop, let this happen—especially since the soon-to-be father was the man she was sworn to protect?